THE WHITE CITY

The White City

Elizabeth Bear

Subterranean Press 2010

First Edition

ISBN: 978-1-59606-323-5

Subterranean Press
PO Box 190106
Burton, MI 48519

www.subterraneanpress.com

for Beth and for Emma

Moscow
Kitai Gorod
May 1903

LADY ABIGAIL IRENE GARRETT gazed up at the rose-colored walls of the Cathedral of the Theophanes and frowned as if its elaborate white gingerbread trim were a personal affront. The creature who observed her held his silence, watching her profile as she craned back her neck. Her cropped hair broke in strands of blond and ash around her collar.

A summery wind blew her open coat wide and unraveled the scarf from her neck so it fluttered behind her like a creamy banner. The reflected stain of sunset across the western sky, the last light of the sun, dyed the silk a shade that might have seemed—to merely mortal eyes—not too dissimilar from the walls of the monastery.

But the creature who watched her was better adapted to noticing subtle color differences by halflight than any living man, and he could pick out layered peaches and vermilions in the sunset that no pigment slapped on a wall could imitate. Oils, in the hands of a master—Chinese red, Alizarin crimson, cadmium yellow—might come close.

"If this is the Chinese City," Abby Irene said dourly, "you might expect a few Chinese persons."

"Forgive me," said the creature, who still sometimes called himself Don Sebastien de Ulloa, though that was only one of the dozens of names he'd worn across the centuries. "Shall I endeavor to have a few imported, or will you content yourself with assurances of postponement? I feel certain an excursion by dirigible to far Cathay should remedy the egregious lack of Chinamen—"

Abby Irene turned her long neck and her shoulders toward him, the corner of her mouth quirking upwards. The gesture made the scandalously unbuttoned collar of her shirtwaist gap, revealing the sorcerer's tattoo tracing a scarlet column of alchemical symbols from her collarbone to vanish between her breasts. The names of quicksilver, white phosphorous, and red arsenic were written over her heart, and the creature—*Sebastien*—knew it for the outward mark of a vow.

He wanted to chase the marks down to the human, living warmth of her belly and drown his senses in the scent of her blood. Whether she read the desire in his face or not, she smiled. "I'll settle for Chinese tea, for the time being. "It's *cold*."

It was a calm night in early summer, but Abby Irene had grown accustomed to the swelter of the new world, and she was no longer a young woman. She felt chills deeply that she would have shrugged off when she lived in London.

"Tea, I think we can find you." Sebastien smiled with closed lips and offered his arm most gallantly.

She took it, tugging her coat closed with the other small hand. "Lead me, my prince."

"I was never a prince."

Her boot nails didn't click on the packed dirt, but that was no reflection on the precision of her stride. She kept up easily; thirty years of detecting made a woman strong, and Abby Irene had never needed to lean on Sebastien's arm. Some day she would; some day he'd bury her, unless she left him first. But now she squeezed his arm with fingers that couldn't dent the dry flesh beneath his shirt and asked, "What were you?"

He ducked his head. "I was prenticed a stonemason."

He hadn't thought the trade of his youth so shocking, but Abby Irene stumbled and let go of his arm to recover her balance, skirts swirling about her ankles. She wobbled a little, but stayed up, and Sebastien kept his hands carefully at his sides.

"Apprenticed," she said.

He nodded. "I think. It was a long time gone, Abby Irene. Memory never grows less fallible. Even for the blood. Especially for the blood. And that, mi corazon, is a kindness."

She had her head cocked aside, that Crown Investigator gleam in her eyes. The scent of her arousal stung him. "You were young."

"Eighteen," he said. "Nineteen. I don't remember exactly." He scrubbed his hands across his face—a gesture for her, a memory of human movement rather than something he felt the need for on his own behalf. "There was a year or two to run on my contract."

She frowned so that he knew all the questions she was not asking—*how did you meet her? Why did you choose to die? Did she even give you a choice?*

What was your name?

He blessed her, that she did not choose to ask them. Instead, she took his arm again and once more fell into step, permitting him to lead her to her requested tea.

The shop he had in mind had been a revolutionary café when he was here last, but times had changed and he imagined so had its clientele. And if not, well—it wasn't as if Abby Irene had never met an anarchist before. Moscow was Europe's most populous city, eight hundred years grown from its humble beginnings, a jewel on the Moskva with its ancient rings of walls, its avenues and cathedrals, its theatres and ballets. Sebastien knew he should have found its earthen streets and horse-drawn streetcars incongruous, but to him they only seemed homey. Comforting: evidence that this city was a city as cities should be.

"This is still not tea," she reminded, as he paused to let a horsecart pass.

He covered her hand with his own. "Follow me. I know just the place."

Because he took them down a side street to avoid a laborers' protest by the university, it was all of twenty minutes before she sat across from him at a linen-covered table, her slim hands cupping a tall glass in a silver holder. The name of the café had not changed—it was still called *Kobalt*—but the clientele he remembered, of painters and poets and young Jack Priest's revolutionary friends talking anarchy over scarred tables—that was gone, replaced by this shabby, gaslit elegance.

And this too shall pass.

Abby Irene leaned forward as if inviting the curls of heat rising from the samovar on her left side to coil through her disarrayed hair. She swirled her tea in the glass and smiled at him. "Thank you. This is lovely."

"And restorative, I hope."

The aroma of tea was pleasant to Sebastien, though he couldn't have said how it might have seemed to a mortal man. He had come to his current state of undeath long before encountering his first infusion of *Camellia sinensis*. But he could also detect the smells of her bread and butter, and of the tablespoon of strawberry jam she had stirred into the hot drink, and *those* nauseated and cloyed.

Human food. So complicated. He drew himself back from his introspection to find Abby Irene gazing at him speculatively.

She pressed a fingertip to the polished silver handle and let the weight of her hand turn the glass. It left no mark on the tablecloth.

Softly, unsettled, Abby Irene said, "There's nowhere in this city I could take you where you have not already been."

"You've never been in Moscow before," Sebastien said, reasonably, wishing she would eat her bread a little faster— or perhaps send it away. But no, she'd need her strength. Better if she dined. "And I have, many times. That wouldn't be any different if I were a human thing."

"But a human thing wouldn't have seen it built stone by stone."

To speak with absolute literal precision, neither had he, but he was willing to allow the metaphor—for its beauty if nothing else. He was glad they had not gone to London. She would have hated having him there, knowing her own native brick and cobble with an intimacy her own life was too short to encompass.

She frowned down at her glass. When her fingers rippled restlessly, a flat silver and garnet band caught the light. Another wampyr would know it for a mark of her allegiance to Sebastien, but seeing it now annoyed him. If you lived long enough, *every* place was equally an exile. But after even a few years in the New World, coming back to the old—with its traditions and elaborations, its codes of conduct and its strictures and its rules—it chafed more than Sebastien had expected.

He was old enough to ignore most of the social niceties. But he wouldn't take risks with the safety of his court. In Europe, Abby Irene—and their friend, Mrs. Phoebe Smith—must go tagged as his property like city dogs.

As if oblivious to his interest, Abby Irene tore off a piece of black bread and tucked it into her mouth. She ate like a princess, meticulous and particular. Sebastien enjoyed watching her: she looked something like a (dowager) princess, too—slender and fair in that English Rose sort of way, with her sleek graying hair cropped fashionably short and the gold-framed spectacles she had just recently overcome her vanity to wear perched on the bridge of her nose.

"It's the curse of a relationship with a more experienced man." Her moment of melancholy seemed to have faded, because she gave him one of her wry half-smiles and picked up her tea. "It gets harder and harder to feign proper naïvete. At my age, I should treasure the opportunity to play the ingénue."

Sebastien let his chin rest on his hand. As he was not dining, he hadn't removed his gloves, but the chill of flesh cooled by the autumn evening outside still permeated gray kid. He thought about what would warm him, watching the light pulse flutter in Abby Irene's lovely throat. It came to Sebastien that he must dine, too, and not from either of his companions—he had drawn from each of them more recently than he liked. Travel was exhausting, and the chill and pallor would not leave his flesh until fresh blood infused it.

Well. Moscow was a cosmopolitan city. And one—as Abby Irene had mentioned so disconsolately—with which he was tolerably familiar. Sebastien tugged at his watch-chain—another antique affectation, and one he needed to rid himself of soon if he meant to stay *au courant*, though he had not quite reconciled himself to wristwatches yet—and opened the case under the table's edge.

Abby Irene set the crust of her bread down on the plate and lifted her chin, stretching skin that began to grow slack. "Poor thing," she said. "You must be starving."

"Moscow has a club," he said. Not an untruth, but a misdirection, and even as he said it he wondered why he felt the need to dissemble. Others lied to their courts, or did not trouble to lie. Sebastien would have preferred to think of his warm companions as—well, as companions. "Several, in fact. Shall I meet you at the ballet?"

She sighed, but it was more affectation than genuine distress. If she were upset in truth, he would have read it in her pulse rate, her respiration, her scent. She lifted one elegant hand, leading with the wrist, and brushed him away with affected disdain. "Go."

"Are you certain?" He glanced over his shoulder, trying to catch the waiter's eye. Abby Irene didn't need his money—certainly not for tea and a slice of bread—but it was a matter of pride to care for one's court.

"Creature of the dark," she intoned, "fly from me. The Moscow nights are brief in May." She hesitated, but could not keep a stern face any longer. Her pink mouth curved. "Seriously, Sebastien. I'll see you in an hour or so. Just don't leave me all alone in my box, or I'll have to seduce some tender scion of minor nobility just to keep up appearances."

Sebastien pushed his chair back and stood. He bowed over Abby Irene's hand and kissed the ring he'd placed there.

« Enchantée, mademoiselle, » he said, and slipped back before the sorcerer could cuff his ear.

Outside the café, the brief summer night still teemed with people. It was a Saturday, and the Muskovites were making the most of mild weather. Lamps flickered on faces and ladies' fashionable hats—the Paris styles of two or three seasons past. Sebastien closed his eyes briefly and breathed deep, bringing the scent of the city within.

He had once known it in his bones. It was not so different now.

Like many cities of an age with the wampyr, Moscow was built in a series of rings. At its heart lay the Moscow Kremlin, the Tsar's residence in his once-capital, a patchwork citadel overlooking the Moskva River. The palaces, arsenals, and churches within its walls made up a crazy-quilt of architecture ranging from the classically Russian elevated proportions of the Church of the Annunciation through the Italian Renaissance façade of the Faceted Hall to the lofty onion domes of the Winter Palace. The previous evening, Abby Irene and Sebastien, prevailing upon Phoebe, and taken her to see and hear the Tsar Bell. Even in her mourning, she had been unable to resist the world's largest bell, which had only been successfully cast through the intervention of imperial sorcerers from the college in Kyiv. Abby Irene had had a great deal to say about the details of the process, and Sebastien hoped that Phoebe had found them as welcome a distraction as had he.

She had been close to Jack.

On the side away from the river, the Kremlin was bounded by Red Square, and beyond that the Kitai Gorod, the Chinese City—which, as Abby Irene had noted, was not Asian in flavor at all. Sebastien was headed in the opposite direction—to the outer ring of fortifications, the Bely Gorod. Moscow's White City, famed for pallid walls and a bohemian arts scene. Russians, Sebastien found— Muscovites in particular—were fanatically devoted to the arts. Sebastien speculated it was cultural memory, a sort of national inferiority complex founded in Russia's late arrival in the Renaissance. Whatever the cause, the outcome appealed to him: the city it produced was vibrant, remarkable—and weird.

Moscow had two or three underground clubs catering to the needs of the blood—the one Sebastien favored was called *Beliye Nochi*, The White Nights, though properly speaking Moscow did not have true white nights as did the Tsar's 200-year-old new capital at Pavelgrad. But he was not bound to Beliye Noche now, unless his other plans bore no fruit.

He had once had friends in Moscow, and evidence suggested he might still.

Six years might seem but an eyeblink to one of the blood, but for a mortal, it could mean the transformation of an entire life. And one's existence *could* change in a relative eyeblink, Sebastien admitted to himself as he threaded between pedestrians on his way to Nikitsky Square. The Bely Gorod once had boasted eleven gates and twenty-eight towers. The wall was no longer complete, but the names of those gates persisted in the squares that had surrounded them.

The woman he meant to see had lived in a building first constructed in the eighteenth century. The scrawled paper in his pocket suggested she might still, and Sebastien could think of no reason other than increasing penury or sudden improbable wealth that might have moved her to relocate. Her name was Irina Stephanova Belotserkovskaya, and she was an artist.

It was Sebastien's unhappy duty to bring her the news of a loved one's death.

He paused at the foot of the stairs leading to her loft. The hallway was a public space, and he required no invitation to enter it, so he told himself that his pause was just the habitual feigning of human windedness. He should have come to see Irina three nights ago, immediately upon his arrival in Moscow. The truth was, he had been stalling, and there were so many small tasks to accomplish that he had managed to delay until Irina's letter of invitation had found *him*.

She must have learned of his arrival through the rumor and report that inevitably passed between those of the blood and those who associated with them, which meant she was still—*affiliated*. That she would send an invitation meant she had not become a member of another wampyr's court, which might mean she still considered herself a part of his.

That would be...convenient. In both the English and Russian senses of the word.

He probably could have distracted himself endlessly in getting himself (and Abby Irene, and Phoebe) installed in the Hotel Bucharest near Red Square, reacquainting himself with the city and finding diversions for the women so they did not spend every waking moment moping over Jack or chasing news of the war for independence now winding to a close in the Americas. Such news was harder to come by here in the East, where distances and languages intervened, and that was in part why Sebastien had chosen to bring them to Russia.

The intervention of the French on the Colonies' side had shortened what could have been a terrible, grinding transatlantic siege—England was not so eager to fight another protracted sea war with *la belle* (and belligerent)

France—but that intervention had come at a price. Abby Irene was unlikely to find herself welcome in her native England again, and none of them could raise much desire to be in Paris after the losses they had suffered there—or to return to an America at war, where Sebastien was presumed dead and if he were not would have a price on his neck. And not the ambulatory sort of death he professed, but the kind that came with flames.

—and this train of thought was bearing him nowhere he cared to travel.

Sebastien steeled himself and ascended the five flights to the topmost floor. Granite steps dished under his feet. The banisters were worn smooth where his gloved hand skipped over them. He did not have to duck under the landing crossbeams, but a man built to more modern proportions might.

Once Sebastien had been tall. In another five hundred years, he imagined he might be accounted a midget, and men would go on hands and knees through buildings such as this.

As he mounted the last flight, a delicious aroma tantalized him. Thick, meaty, it brought the rush of saliva to his cold mouth and a chill to the pit of his stomach.

Blood, and human, and more than a little.

Irina Stephanova's loft was the only apartment on the top floor. She had been a friend, and when Sebastien paused to listen through the panel and heard nothing within, he felt as if a dagger twisted within him. The smell of blood was fresh, but not *too* fresh—an hour or two old, surely. Perhaps three.

He put a hand on the knob. The door was locked. Nothing moved within.

He broke the lock without straining and let the door swing wide, the shattered knob hanging on its broken linkages. Inside, Irina Stephanova's one-room loft lay dark except for what light filtered up through high northern windows from the gaslamps at street level, and what moonlight fell through mildew-stained skylights. It would not have been enough for human eyes, but from where he paused just outside the door Sebastien could see plainly.

Irina had hung sailcloth across the eastern windows to shut out the glare. Candles had dripped, run, and guttered dark on two of three paint-stained bureaus pushed against the walls. Sebastien smelled the cold acrid reek of charred wick: a kerosene lantern had burned itself out as well. A palette of oils lay discarded on dropcloths covering the corner of the room that got the best daylight, smears of pigment adding a rich, bitter undernote to the loft's collage of smells. A slashed canvas—a female nude, Sebastien thought, though the details were distorted by the defacement— was propped upon an easel.

The dead woman sprawled before it, a canvas knife congealing into the same puddle of blood in which she lay.

Sebastien crossed the floor to her, stepping carefully. He experienced no difficulty in entering the loft: he had often been Irina Stephanova's invited guest. He crouched beside the body, removed his glove, and reached across the sticky puddle to brush blood-clotted black hair from her cheek.

In the process, he learned two things. One was that the dead woman was not yet cold, though cooling. The other was that she was not Irina Stephanova.

He heard the treads on the stair, saw the scanning beams of electric torches and heard rough male voices that made no effort at concealment. The wampyr stood, turning away from the body. It would have been easy enough to vanish through a window, and for a moment Sebastien considered it. It was the only way he could manage to keep his date with Abby Irene for the midnight ballet.

But remaining here would give him a route of access to the investigation. And perhaps to Irina Stephanova, to whom he now wished even more strongly to speak.

Two men stepped back and one stepped up into the doorway. The one who put himself forward was a slight creature, slim-shouldered, silhouetted against bright lights.

Sebastien tugged his glove back on. He spoke in Russian, so there would be no confusion.

—Good evening. By your presence, I presume the blood has dripped through to the tenants below?

—Don't tell me.— The slender man said. —There's a perfectly reasonable explanation for your being here.

In the heart of the Kremlin, the massive Tsar Bell began—sonorous, savage—to toll the eleventh hour.

Moscow
Bely Gorod
January 1897

THE SNOW HAD SETTLED over Moscow in October, and would not melt entirely until perhaps March. It creaked and moaned underfoot, heaped so high where it had been shoveled against walls that the ground-floor dwellers carved tunnels to let light in their windows—but it kept the heat of coal fires snug inside, though the pale stone of the old city's eponymous medieval walls showed it filthy and trodden by comparison.

Teamsters came after every storm and stood by shaggy, stolid horses while workmen in wool and furs and quilting heaved shovelfuls of snow into their carts. Once each load had settled the wagon bed toward the axles, the carters hauled it to the river, where it lay piled atop the ice in drifts like haystacks until a thaw.

Jack Priest had spent enough of his short life traveling to adapt readily to most climates, but even he had to admit that this was extreme—especially after summering at Sebastien's home in Spain. Sebastien had offered to leave him behind when he came to Moscow for a winter holiday, but Jack would rather endure the cold than be parted from his patron for four months, and so he wrapped himself in jumpers and coats and tugged sable caps down over his ears—and still the cold found crevices to work through. It pried at the hems of his clothing as if it had fingers and a malevolent sense of humor, and somehow managed to get icy hands down his neck, up his sleeves, across the small of his back.

But the cold couldn't keep him inside, though he learned to move like the Muscovites did: shoulders hunched and chin tucked, scurrying with short quick strides that kept one's feet solidly planted even on slick terrain and didn't kick open the skirts of one's coat to let the wind inside. He muffled his neck and face in scarves and wondered how peculiar he would look if he began affecting goggles. Or perhaps a full facemask—something to shield his eyes and the skin around them without interrupting his view of Moscow.

Because Moscow was worth looking at. A wampyr's paramour by necessity became a bit nocturnal, but the truth was that Moscow in January was not just cold, but dark. Jack could have managed to navigate the city entirely in Sebastien's company simply by napping through the brief daylight. But then, he reasoned, he would never learn Russian.

And he'd never have witnessed the weighty domes of the Church of St. Catherine the Great Martyr in-the-Fields with the cold winter sky behind them. A sight that was worth a little walking out alone.

Besides, the young Russian girls were different from their Western sisters. He might say wilder, except it wasn't wildness, precisely. *Freedom*, that was the word. They went about unchaperoned and loose-haired, and they had opinions and educations more rigorous than those encouraged in the West. Russia and Britain had been at the edge of war for decades, each thwarting the others' imperial ambitions, and so they also found an Englishman—even a pretend-Englishman like Jack—unbearably exotic.

When he was fourteen, Sebastien had provided to him the means for complete independence. Jack was both emancipated and self-reliant, and Sebastien had made it plain that he considered Jack perfectly capable of seeing to his own maintenance and entertainment. Having been raised a companion of the blood, however, Jack found his tastes ran to the more mundane. He liked tea bars and coffee houses, the sorts where the floors were gritty and the raw wood pillars hung with peeling onionskin layers of cheaply printed flyers.

Today, Jack let his footsteps lead him to a café called Kobalt, a half-underground maze of mismatched tables and chairs scattered with even more mismatched furniture that one reached by descending a steep iron stair across from a building whose windows were plastered with political posters that Jack couldn't read more than every other word of. He recognized the anarchist's symbol across some, the red-white-and-black two-color process giving the whole a bold look. The whole business made him itch with a funny liquid craving, not too different from looking at girls.

Jack paused at the top of the stair and sniffed deeply. He smelled eggs, fresh black bread, beans and potatoes, the tang of cheese or sour cream. In other words, lunch, or—for someone who slept into the afternoon, as a wampyr's companion might be wont—a very nice breakfast.

When Jack entered, the café was already thickening with a crowd. He'd only been here once before, midmorning, and hadn't found it quite so infested with people. Now, full—while the walls weren't quite bulging—it gave off quite a different air. Jack walked into a low, shadowy space full of the hum of conversation he couldn't follow, the smells of tea and coffee from assorted pots and samovars. The selection of food looked limited—Jack imagined this was more a sitting-and-sipping kind of place than one of renown for its cuisine—but what there was smelled promising.

He slid into the middle of three empty stools at the bar. When the stocky blue-eyed counterman turned around, Jack ordered coffee by the pot, scalded milk, the eggs, and two slices of quick bread studded with berries. The bread arrived first, rewarding his strategy, and Jack began the serious business of lining his stomach while somewhere in the back of the kitchen, protein sizzled.

The coffee came in a silver-colored pot with a rustic mug for decanting into and drinking from. The milk steamed in a jug. Jack lifted coffee in his right hand and milk in the left, pouring both simultaneously into red stoneware. The rich, brown scent, mellowed by dairy sweetness, rose on coils of steam. The first sip floated him on a bubble of well-being. He closed his eyes and sighed, hands caged loosely around his cup.

When he opened them, a girl was looking at him side-long through the veil of her hair. She had her head ducked down, one fingernail picking at the grout between the blue tiles of the counter. He noticed flecks of crimson and gold under the nail and embedded in her cuticle, freckling the sleeve of her blouse. She wore trousers and a man's coat and waistcoat, and with her wire-smooth black locks and her eyes like oilstones resting on the ledges of her pale brown cheeks she seemed unbearably exotic to Jack.

She smiled at him and said, "You are the Englishman."

Jack assembled his expression—blank with shock, by the numb feeling of his face—into something more welcoming. "I'm Jack Priest," he said, and thrust his hand out to shake hers as if she were a man.

"Irina Stephanova," she answered, leaving off her last name in favor of a patronymic, an informal fashion he was becoming accustomed to.

She couldn't have been much older than he—two years or three—but she had the lean wariness of somebody who's used to looking out for herself. "I hope you'll tell me what I did to attract such welcome attention, so I can make a habit of it."

She squinted slightly, head cocked forward, and after a moment shook her head self-deprecatingly. "My English—" she explained, and waved over her shoulder. "You sit with my friends and with me, please?"

Following the gesture of her head, he noticed a group of three other girls about the same age gathered around a samovar on a low table. Each was dressed in similarly Bohemian splendor. Though none of them were in drag, all were uncorseted, wearing blouses, shawls, and sweaters layered loose over long wool skirts. One wore fingerless gloves, a not-unreasonable affectation given the chill in the basement café.

—I'm waiting for my breakfast,— Jack offered. His Russian wasn't much better than her English, but it was often easier to understand somebody fumbling through your language than zooming past in their own.

—Dmitri will bring it,— she said, with a nod to the counterman. Jack turned in time to see the look Dmitri sent back in his turn, intense, focused, leavened by a slight smile. Possessive, perhaps, but Jack didn't get a sense that Irina Stephanova was impressed by the possessiveness, if she had even noticed it.

Jack smiled politely as Irina Stephanova swiped his coffeepot and milk jug, leaving him little choice other than to cause a scene or to carry the mug along after her, balancing the half-eaten plate of bread atop it. She led him over to the cluster of worn leather couches centered on a glass-topped coffee table where her friends were sitting, and hip-checked one of her girlfriends over to make room. When Jack settled beside her, all blushes and apologies, he couldn't edge over far enough to keep from feeling the radiant heat of her body against his thigh.

Dmitri was probably going to spit in his eggs.

Irina Stephanova settled his coffee and milk on the table with a clatter, edging aside used cups and plates dotted with crumbs to do so. Pointing quickly, she introduced the young women surrounding her, and it was all Jack could do to catch the proper names. Patronymics were on their own reconnaissance. Fortunately, nobody else in the café seemed too determined to enforce their use, and for Jack—already feeling transgressive in using the Christian names of people, of *women*, he barely knew—one more revolutionary increment came easy.

The one in the red sweater, mahogany-brown hair piled high, was Svetlana. She had frayed shirt-cuffs splattered with motheaten yellow stains that looked like the residue of some mild acid, and her knuckles were marked with a fine lacework of scratches. He was unsurprised to hear Irina Stephanova identify her as a sculptress.

The heavyset one with medium-brown hair, wearing a sort of embroidered robe that seemed inspired by kimono or caftan over her dress, was Tania. She was drinking black tea from a ruby-tinted glass, heavy costume rings glinting on her fingers.

—Tania works in gouache,— Irina Stephanova said. —And this is Nadia.

The third woman was a redhead, neither flaming carrot nor auburn but a soft gingery color, the locks cropped off at her shoulders and oiled in soft springy curls. She was the one in a goat's-hair shawl, the open lacework slipping down her shoulders. She smiled widest at Jack as he sipped his coffee and leaned forward to set the mug down.

"So you are the Englishman." Her accent was meticulous.

"Someone has to be."

She laughed and quickly translated for the others, who laughed as well. Irina Stephanova looked over her shoulder at him, flipping her long black hair out of the way. "Jack, you are artist?"

He shook his head. "A dilettante." Coffee was an excuse not to answer the question in too detailed a fashion. "But I prefer the company of artists to that of polite society, and in general I find the feeling is mutual." He repeated himself, as best as he could, in Russian, for Tania and Svetlana.

His breakfast arrived then, a welcome excuse to drop out of the conversation to listen. "It's all right," Irina said to Jack as Dmitri vanished back behind the counter. "He is not artist either, but wishes he was. We put up with him."

Jack smiled and stuffed his face with bread and eggs. He'd always had a good facility for languages—an indispensable talent for anyone spending time in the company of an itinerant vampire—and he knew before too long if he kept up the exposure he'd be dreaming in Russian. Also, it was somehow restful to sit at the table with the women and listen to them gossip about critics and galleries and fellow artists, veering off occasionally to brush over revolutionary politics. Leaning back into the embrace of the couch, balancing his plate on his knee, he relaxed and ate and concentrated on understanding as much of the talk as he could follow.

By the time he'd finished his breakfast and was making a few more hesitant conversational overtures, the café was packed to overflowing. Despite the fact that Jack had not seen them here on his last visit, Irina Stephanova and her friends were apparently a part of the regular clientele—at least, judging by the number of people who wandered over to greet them as part of the ritual of entering the space. Kobalt was not just the hangout of artists and Republicans, but the usual associated crowd of musicians, anarchists, nihilists, and students.

Jack's coffee was still hot enough for drinking, so he refilled his cup and settled back in. The women seemed to have accepted his presence—there was something to be said for not monopolizing the conversation—and now he felt he was getting to see their real faces. *That* was something he almost never witnessed when he was with Sebastien, because almost everyone who encountered Sebastien wanted something from him—his help, in his guise as the Great Detective; his attention, as an elder of the blood; his friendship or his patronage or his destruction.

The short afternoon passed pleasantly enough. The winter sun was lowering and Jack thinking of making his excuses when three men about the same age as Irina Stephanova and her friends wandered over with the peculiar insouciant slouch of boys desperately attempting to appear casual before girls. Jack forced himself not to frown over the introductions—not because he minded the competition, but because more names and faces abruptly felt like overload. Still, he managed to sort out that the tall dark-haired one with the charismatic stare was Ilya, and that he was a painter by night and a tailor's piecer by day. The two medium-tall ones with medium-brown hair and gray eyes (one plump and one thin) were Sacha and Grigor, and they were brothers.

"Be careful what you say to them," Irina Stephanova whispered. —Ilya said their father is a policeman, and they might be agitators.

Or it might be adolescent rebellion against a figure in authority. But Jack wasn't going to say so with his out loud voice.

One was a poet and one was a painter, but Jack was damned if he could remember which was which within thirty seconds of the introduction. It bothered him a little, because they seemed at pains to distinguish themselves from one another, and Sebastien would have known—and known a dozen other things about them simply by observation, within the space of that same half a minute.

Jack was practicing that trick of mindfulness, but he did not find it easy.

He watched as the boys—Sacha, the plump one, was plainly the ringleader—eased up on the girls with the idea of going to a labor organizer's meeting, and tried to use Sebastien's methods as he did. Sacha had a better job, he thought, because his shoes might be carefully scuffed but they were also sound and just as carefully repaired, and all of the shiny patches on his coat looked cosmetic.

Grigor, the thin one, revealed himself to be the painter after all, through the simple expedient of being unable to stop talking about a gallery showing planned for the following day. They all spoke rapid-fire in Russian, with occasional forays into vestigial English and Czech for Jack's benefit, while Jack followed as well as he could.

—You will come to the union meeting with us?—Sacha asked Jack, so suddenly it took two seconds' thought before Jack understood him.

Jack shook his head. —I am meeting a friend for dinner.

Beside him, Irina Stephanova seemed to have grown bored with the conversation. Jack watched as she filled her glass with concentrated tea, diluted it with hot water from the samovar, and glanced over her shoulder before producing a flask that Jack had already learned contained brandy.

"They speak of my showing. You will come to that?" she said, leaning sideways to speak into his ear without disturbing the main flow of discussion. "You get in without paying."

He held out his empty coffee cup, and she splashed brandy into the bottom. He touched his lips to it, the fumes stinging his eyes to watering. A fashionable gallery show was quite an accomplishment for an artist not yet twenty. And a woman artist at that.

—I will come. Tell me please, what time,— he answered in Russian, so she would laugh at his accent.

Arrangements were made, and he accepted the free pass she handed him, her fingertips brushing his palm.

He made sure to wave at Dmitri on the way out, just to watch him glower.

Moscow
Bely Gorod
May 1903

—I HAVE IN MY pocket a letter from the woman who
lives here requesting my attendance,— Sebastien said.
He spread his arms and raised his hands. For a moment,
he thought of giving the pseudonym he had traveled under—*Doctor John Nast*—but the note tucked into his coat
was addressed to *My dear Don Sebastien*, and explanations
could become so complicated.

The slender-shouldered figure that had stepped forward now withdrew between the other two in the doorway,
opening a gap that a man could pass through.

—Come out slowly, please.— he said. The same voice
as before, by which Sebastien inferred he must be in charge.

Sebastien obeyed, hands still raised. Upon returning
to the hallway and the dull gaslight therein, he could quite
clearly make out the details of all three Imperial Police. The
one he'd identified as the leader was fiftyish and clad in
wrinkled mufti, a rumpled brown coat and ill-tied tie so

cliché that the wampyr badly hoped it was an affectation. His hair was almost the same dull shade as the coat, or if anything a little mousier, and he wore small square spectacles that caught the light.

His subordinates were a mismatched team, despite their uniforms. One was tall and slender; the other of medium height and muscular build, gray-eyed where the first was dark. Though they were armed, Sebastien did not expect to find them much of a threat. He still remained at pains to prevent them from discovering his disregard. Truly, it would be better for everyone if this could be resolved—cooperatively.

—I am called Don Sebastien de Ulloa, and the woman on the floor is not our hostess.

The detective's eyes narrowed, his pulse accelerating— and it had already been quite speedy, considering his recent run up the stairs and confrontation with an unknown murder suspect. Sebastien had no doubt he recognized the name. Notoriety had its price.

—You are the so-called Great Detective?

Sebastien nodded.

—I am Gospadin Dyachenko, Imperial Inspector. Do you have some proof of your identity?

—A passport,— Sebastien answered.

—Give the passport and the letter you mentioned to Sergeant Asimov.

Dyachenko nodded to the taller and thinner of the uniformed officers, and Sebastien provided the paperwork with, he thought, a good show of cheerful cooperation and no mention of the three hundred-ruble banknotes tucked carelessly inside the folds of paper. He could have afforded more, but he judged that an inappropriately large gratuity would only encourage suspicion.

The sergeant withdrew, riffling papers under the hallway light. Sebastien saw his hand go to his pocket before he handed the papers to his sturdier companion, who still had a pistol trained on Sebastien. He too checked them over, and then provided the lot to Dyachenko, who stuffed them in his inside pocket unexamined.

—Of course, You will accompany us, Don Sebastien.

—Of course. It's no more than I expected,— Sebastien said. —Only I wonder could you have someone deliver a message to my lady friend? Apparently, I'm about to stand her up for the ballet.

Moscow
Bely Gorod
January 1897

THE NEXT DAY BROUGHT Jack out into another particularly fine, particularly wintry afternoon, the clear sky above brilliant as blue spinel, the sun splinter-sharp off the white walls of Moscow's ancient fortress heart. The gallery—his destination—nestled against the inner wall of the Bely Gorod. The palm Irina Stephanova—Belotserkovskaya, her last name was on the invitation—had touched tingled inside his glove as he handed his card to the gray-coated gentleman at the door and was allowed inside. As Jack strode past incomprehensible posters in the entry, he was not surprised by the lack of a milling crowd. Anyone sensible would be inside already, where there might be vodka and nibbles. And how many people could you expect at an unknown artist's opening, after all?

When he tugged the interior door ajar, his eyes provided the answer: rather a few more than expected. Sight lines in the space were disrupted by a maze of two-thirds height display walls and only three or four people were immediately obvious, but warm, moist air and the murmur of voices spoke of a significant number of people just out of sight. A glance at the canvases hanging on those walls and the sculptures studding plinths told him that not all of them were there for Irina Stephanova, unless she managed an unlikely juxtaposition of art styles and media.

A coat check girl hurried to relieve Jack of his cold-weather armor, which he shed gratefully. The layers that proved so necessary outside were stifling within. It seemed that he'd scarcely handed over his coat when a glass of vodka replaced it in his hand, and a moment later a tray of blini laden with chopped egg and sour cream drifted past. No caviar, but that might have been a bit much to hope for. He folded a tender buckwheat crepe into his mouth with no complaints.

Irina Stephanova appeared at his left side. Her complexion concealed any flush, but by the brightness of her eyes the glass of vodka in her fingers was not her first. He bowed over her unburdened hand and kissed the air above it, so as not to leave behind lingering egg crumbs.

Nevertheless, she giggled. "Gospodin Priest, is good of you to come."

"Miss—Belot...Belotserk..." An Englishman would have stumbled, and so Jack did too, though he was Czech by birth and had spent two years of his childhood in the most cosmopolitan of possible surroundings: the wampyr crèche from which Sebastien had purchased him.

She laughed. "Irina Stephanova," she said. "Are we not friends now?"

"Then you must call me Jack," he replied. "Surely these are not all yours?"

She collected and dismissed someone's life's work with a scoop and flip of her hand. "This crap?" She lingered over the English word as if it pleased her, childlike, delighted by her own temerity. Rolling the R as if letting it breathe out its essence across her tongue. "This is Ilya's."

Jack winced. It wasn't bad, honestly—certainly not such *crap* as she characterized it. Still lifes, figure studies, a Moscow street scene with gray rain slanting across unpaved highways and one lone figure in a red coat just about to vanish around a building in the distance. "I wonder where he's going."

Irina sipped her vodka. "Probably to loo," she said, and when Jack laughed, half-unwilling, "I know. I am mean woman."

"Mean, funny woman," he agreed.

She flashed her eyes at him over the lip of her glass.

"Who else is here?"

She took his arm, guiding him through the small white rooms. Filtered electric light—still rare in Moscow—cast shadowless illumination. He stopped to examine a bronze of a starved horse, its prickery mane thinning and bones staring through its scratched-dull coat. "Svetlana," she said.

Jack smiled. "This is all your friends?"

She hesitated, releasing his elbow, and he wondered if perhaps he should not have used the word *friends*. But after a moment, she nodded crisply. —Yes. All. Grigor, darling.

Grigor turned, startled. He was drinking white wine, which Jack thought a strange choice for the bleak mid-winter, and it splashed high in the glass. He didn't spill it, though, and once he identified Irina, a broad grin broke across his face, revealing teeth stained with tea and streaked from the Russian habit of drinking it with sugar cubes clenched between them. —Sweetheart!

He reached out to her, a hand showing the pale band of a missing ring taking her shoulder and drawing her into a one-armed embrace while the other hand lifted his wine glass aside. Irina secured against his hip like a docked ship, he turned his attention to Jack. —And…Excuse me please, how are you called?

"Jack," Jack said. "Jack Priest." He extended a hand, amused to watch Grigor shuffle drink and girl until he could clasp it. —Congratulations on your show.

Grigor beamed. —A friend made it possible. A patron. He arranged the show.

He seemed to be watching Jack carefully when he said it, and Jack was not imagining the glare with which Irina favored Grigor. *The missing ring.* Grigor was a courtesan of the blood, or (given his naked hand) he had been, and Irina—disapproved? It bore watching.

—Your pieces are very good,— Jack said, latching on to the excuse not to stare Grigor in the face any longer.

Grigor's style had something of an impressionist air, deeply saturated colors and great senses of place and air, billowing crags upon billowing skies. —Where is this? This is not near Moscow,— Jack asked, pointing to one long landscape that showed a gray cliff stark above blue water, scaling to an azure sky.

—Kjerag. Norway.— Grigor smiled. —Doesn't it make you wish that you could fly?

Jack nodded, dry-mouthed—Grigor had captured some sense of the grandeur of the place, and when he looked up the artist was smiling.

—Is your brother here?— Jack asked, because it seemed polite, and he didn't catch Irina's wince and shake of her head until a moment too late.

But Grigor only winced too. —I am afraid Sacha prefers not to attend such things. But I will pass along that you thought of him.

There is something about this that Sacha does not approve of, Jack translated. He kept his expression mild.

"Thank you," Jack said, as Irina extricated herself from Grigor's embrace and came around to take his arm again. "Have a good evening."

Grigor seemed all smiles again as they left, but Jack was shaking his head. "I guess I put my foot in it that time."

Irina stared at him blankly. "Put your...foot?"

"Was rude," Jack clarified. She backed away, frowning. He didn't think he knew how to express it in Russian, but the expression suddenly flashed to mind. "Nye kulturni."

"Is family fight," she said, with a shrug. "Nothing for you to know."

Another gesture swept him up into her train. Jack smiled and followed through scattered men and women, singles and duos and small conversational knots. Irina Stephanova led him past the bar, where she refilled her own glass and procured one for him.

"Hey," Jack said. When he had Irina Stephanova's attention, he indicated a taller man with his eyes. "Is that Dmitri the waiter?"

She waved him away. —He paints. Not very well. He has nothing in this show.— Then she paused, and said grudgingly, "No passion, but technically proficient, I suppose. I did not tell you this, but—for lousy painter, he is very good forger."

Jack made a face of surprise, and she grinned at him. "Forger?"

She shrugged. "Man must eat. He has elderly mother. Café does not pay very well, truly or no?"

Svetlana and Tania stood alongside them there—a brief relief, given Svetlana's excellent English, but after a moment they turned away, summoned by a photographer to stand in front of one of Svetlana's sculptures—a weary-looking woman, this time, her skirts rent about the hem.

Jack watched, a bit bedazzled, as Svetlana bent Tania's head back and kissed her for the camera, long and with apparent sincerity.

He raised his eyebrows at Irina.

Her expression as she handed him a glass of vodka could not have been more bland. "You are offended?"

"Not at all," he said. A childhood spent in a wampyr crèche did not leave one easily open to shock. "Only a little surprised by their openness."

Irina smiled. "They are surprising, yes."

Jack gestured to Svetlana's sculpture—wonderful, evocative, broken-spirited. "Does she make anything happy?"

Irina's laugh was all in her eyes. "She is Russian." She lifted her glass against his and intoned, — Na zdrovyeh.

—Na zdrovyeh.— Jack held the glass cupped left-handed, fumes stinging his eyes, and touched it to his lips just enough to let the unfamiliar sweet fire shimmer across his palate. Irina Stephanova seemed to be watching for his reaction, so he showed one—arched eyebrows and a gasp.

"Your first time?"

He nodded. He'd more sniffed than tasted the brandy the previous day. Nobody on the continent thought much of a young man taking beer or wine once in a while, and Sebastien less so than most. But Jack was ill-experienced with harsher spirits...or, to consider the subtext of Irina Stephanova's question, with women. Sebastien protected his ward fiercely. Perhaps a little too fiercely, Jack thought, now

that he was full sixteen years and—by most standards—
a man.

Old enough to die in a war. Old enough to walk
abroad in Europe's war-weary cities unchaperoned. Not
old enough for Sebastien to accept as a full-on member of
his court, however.

If I bring home a lover, Jack thought, *he'll pretty much
have to admit I'm grown.* His own ulterior motive shamed
him and the lingering tingle of Irina's remembered touch
still warmed his palm; surely there were better reasons to
want to know a pretty girl than using her to get into the bed
of a thousand-year-old living dead man.

A pretty girl with skill, Jack amended, as they came
around another set of baffles and Irina Stephanova stopped,
eyes bright, obviously waiting for his reaction. The walls
on the left and the right sides held canvases of moderate
size, but Jack did not register the subject matter beyond a
riot of color and texture. He could not pull his eyes away
from the wall before him, where one great square unframed
canvas hung with three smaller but similarly propor-
tioned stacked each above another to its right. The image
spread across all four seemed at first glance abstract, streaks
and thicknesses of China reds and cobalt blues and the livid
twilight purple they became when combined—*poison*, Jack
thought, with the fragment of his mind that was doing
anything except perceiving—but then he saw that it was
a sunset, the silhouette of a wrecked ship canted on rocks

before it dominating the lowest of the small canvases, its twisted masts and spars tilting to punctuate the lower right-hand corner of the great one.

Jack felt as if something in the painting reached out and closed fiery fingers around his heart.

—You painted these?

She could have taken offense, but instead she nodded, eyes dancing with silent laughter.

—You are a prodigy.— He wondered what she would think of Sebastien de Ulloa—wampyr, hobbyist detective, peculiar old soul.

Irina Stephanova sipped her vodka. "It will take one to know one. That is the English idiom, yes?"

—Yes.— Jack smiled. He could not have said which of her comments he was answering. He tasted the vodka again, instead: it went down smoother this time. He stole a glance at her soft, cold-cracked lower lip and wondered if he had the courage to kiss it, as Svetlana had kissed Tania. The image brought a fresh flush of heat through him, a tightening and prickling of private skin.

Kissing Irina—Not here, of course, in front of her admirers. But maybe a little later, over coffee and pastries in some café that did not cater to nihilists and revolutionaries.

He wondered what she would taste like. Girl, of course, but how did girls taste?

Okay, maybe he was interested in some things in addition to proving his adulthood to Sebastien.

He was still wondering about that when she raised her gaze to glance over his shoulder and stiffened. Jack had seen that expression often enough on courtiers— never those of Sebastien's court, but those of the courts of other brothers and sisters of the blood—to know before he turned that whoever approached behind him, it was somebody who played predator to Irina Stephanova's prey. He stepped away from her and turned, to meet the enemy face to face.

Or face to lapel, rather. To say that Jack was not tall would be a kind understatement; Irina Stephanova had inches as well as years on him, and she was no giantess. So the man who had come up behind Jack didn't need to be tall to tower over him.

But it helped.

—Sergei Nikolaevich,— Irina Stephanova said, squaring her shoulders. —I did not invite you.

Whatever Sergei Nikolaevich answered it was in Russian too fast and blurred for Jack to follow, but Jack took the opportunity of his speech to examine the man's face. He was young, not too much older than Irina, with the colorless hair and gray complexion that Jack had thought of as iconically Russian until he came here and saw what the people actually looked like.

He wore a black felted wool suitcoat with a Mandarin collar, Milan fashion from three years previous and so all the rage in Moscow now. Pocked slabs of cheek hung over it, ending in a stern jaw that was currently elevated in belligerence. His eyes were filmed and dull. He looked ill or impassioned or perhaps very drunk—waxy, sweating, fine locks of hair adhered to his forehead, with all the blood fallen out of his face. He weaved a little on his feet, but public drunkenness was no surprise in a Moscow winter.

Jack understood what Irina said, however—perhaps because she spoke so slowly and clearly: —His canvases are at the other end of the building. Someone can direct you. What a pity *you* didn't have anything selected this time. Was Starkad tired of you?

She began to turn away until Sergei Nikolaevich dropped a neatly manicured hand on her sleeve. He swayed, but Jack couldn't detect the reek of alcohol on him. Possibly the vodka Jack had drunk had destroyed his own sense of smell.

Irina glared at the hand and Jack stepped forward.

"Pardon me," he said in English, trusting his tone to carry the intention. "I don't think the lady likes that."

Sergei Nikolaevich puffed up like a mastiff, but before he could do or say whatever he was working himself up to Irina pushed his hand off her arm and stepped back. Now what she said was low and snaky, and Jack couldn't follow it. But either Irina's words, Jack's glare, or the fact that they were drawing a crowd was enough to make Sergei withdraw, headshaking, back the way he had come. Irina watched him go, puffed up like a cat that has just stared down a big dog, breathing high and tight through her nose.

—Boyfriend?— Jack asked, when he was out of earshot.

Irina shook herself out of her half-trance. Ruefully, she looked at the glass of vodka in her hand. It had mostly spilled over her fingers, but she knocked back what was left. With his own glass, Jack imitated her. Head spinning, he regretted it.

"He...he *wishes*? He wishes so. But with you as my hero, I do not worry, no?" She touched his wrist, fingers hooking to beckon him along without ever actually quite taking hold of him.

—Come.

Bemused, he came. She led him around another baffled half-wall—he left his empty glass on a waiter's tray—through a back door, and into a secluded corner in the cold, darkening areaway behind the gallery. There—while he was still wondering what to do and what to say—she kissed him on the mouth most thoroughly.

She was just as soft and scratchy and wonderful as Jack had anticipated. Her lips were dry and she stung with vodka, and after a moment her tongue started to pry at his teeth so he opened them to let her in. When she pulled back, he put one hand on her nape so she didn't go too far. In a poem, her lips would have been Chinese red as well, vermilion as the sunset sprawled across her canvases, but they were pale sienna like eggshells. He felt a tingle on his neck, as if someone were observing them, but just this once he did not turn to check. It was more important to watch her smile when she said, "It was boring party anyway. Come with me?"

Wordless, he nodded. And did.

Moscow
Police Palace, Kremlin
May 1903

As Asimov led Sebastien into a paint-peeling beige interview room, undecorated except for the high enameled tin ceiling and the patterns of rust surrounding the cold radiator, there was no indication that the officer considered him anything other than an honored guest. Sebastien breathed a sigh of relief when he saw that the interview room had no external windows. It was a trick meant to keep detainees ignorant of the passing of time, but in Sebastien's case it would serve as a protection. He had no need to immediately inform his arresting officers that he was a dead man if there were no threat of exposure to the sun.

Although the Tsar's government would never admit it, Moscow's Imperial Police were modeled on London's force, and Sebastien found the procedures of his detention tolerably familiar. He thought we would be allowed to cool his heels for an hour or two, and then, when the investigator had obtained as much information about Sebastien and the crime as he could dig up quickly and the interview subject had had time to work himself into a lather, Dyachenko would be in to commence the questioning. Additionally, Sebastien had as much as insured that he would first question Abby Irene. Which was a little like sending a kitten to interview a tiger, but Sebastien could not bring himself to feel too troubled by it.

Sebastien had resources that most mortal detainees would not. Where a typical human would wear himself out fussing at the metaphorical bars of his cage, Sebastien merely selected his chair—the wooden one by the table that was patently intended to be his—and settled himself, hands folded, for the wait. The sounds of conversation drifted to him from the offices outside, men and a few women going about their business in the usual way of police stations.

As he let himself drift, Sebastien could hear their footsteps, their heartbeats, the pattern by which the doors throughout the offices opened and closed. He could hear the small noises the building made, as well—its foundations settling, its stone walls shedding the heat of the sun, its old dry wood contracting in the chill. Most of the conversation he could discern was about the factory strike, though a little pertained to the murder. Before too long he heard a pair of familiar voices and allowed himself a smile.

There was more than enough here to hold his attention for weeks, if he let it. He was only just getting to know the place when newly familiar footsteps approached, a key turned in the lock, and the door of the interview room swung wide enough to admit the slender frame of Imperial Inspector Dyachenko. He closed it behind him, and Sebastien could hear that someone locked them in. Dangerous for Dyachenko, if Sebastien had been of a mind to be difficult—but it was a show of trust, all in the spirit of building rapport, and the wampyr chose to accept it as such.

Dyachenko dragged a chair over, its rough pine legs skipping across worn taupe tiles, and plunked down into it. He produced Sebastien's passport from inside his coat, as if it had never left the pocket, and set it on the table between them. The letter of invitation was nowhere in sight, but Sebastien had not expected to see it again unless he were being confronted with it. It was, after all, evidence in a murder investigation.

Dyachenko rested his fingertips on the passport but did not push it across the table. He tapped them once, twice, and cleared his throat. His spectacles flashed back the gaslight when he tipped his head back.

—So who was the dead woman?

—A most direct opening gambit, Imperial Inspector.— Sebastien shrugged and continued, —I do not know. She was already dead when I made her acquaintance.

—The coroner estimates two to three hours,— Dyachenko said.

—So do I. Should you be providing so much information to a suspect?

The detective tilted his head to one side and smiled.

—Don Sebastien, your whereabouts in the hour before sunset?

—My room in the Hotel Bucharest, preparing for the ballet. My companions, Dr. Garrett and Mrs. Smith, can confirm my whereabouts at that time. As can a valet provided by the hotel, who assisted with my dressing. Mikhail Gregorovich, I believe the young man's name to be.

Sebastien kept himself still, waiting the next question. It came, slightly surprisingly, in perfectly excellent English. "And then there is the small matter, Don Sebastien, of your allergy to sunlight, is there not?"

"It would have kept me indoors at that time," Sebastien allowed, with an incline of his head not unlike the one with which Dyachenko had earlier graced him.

"Setting aside for the moment motive and opportunity, there is also the issue of means," Dyachenko continued. He raked nibbled fingers through his mouse-colored hair. "It would be most unusual for a wampyr to slaughter an unarmed woman with a canvas knife, and even more unusual for that wampyr to show signs of hunger and deprivation when arrested mere hours later, when there is no indication that he had been injured in the struggle. Not to mention the waste of all that blood."

"And all that life," Sebastien answered.

He thought he sounded only slightly reproachful, but Dyachenko's eyebrows rose. "Do you know the whereabouts of Irina Stephanova Belotserkovskaya?"

—I do not,— Sebastien said. Although he appreciated the gesture, Russian was really no more trouble to him than English; all tongues were equally foreign in this age.

—Your women have come to collect you.— Dyachenko rose from his chair. He left the passport stranded on the table, a paper shoal on a scarred wooden sea. —You should hurry: the sunrise is quite soon. I hope you and the formidable Doctor Garrett will be willing to make yourselves available to assist in the investigation.

—I cannot imagine anything we would like better. Irina Stephanova is a friend.

That smile of Dyachenko's was really something else, if you looked closely. It went all the way back in his eyes.

He gave Sebastien another one before he turned away and rapped for an open door. A man with enough gall, or enough trust—or little enough sense of self-preservation— to turn his back on a wampyr. Interesting.

As Dyachenko left the room, Sebastien lifted the passport from the table and feathered the pages with his thumb. Tucked inside the folder was a calling card in the name of Yuri Danylevich Dyachenko, bearing the address of this police station and two telephone numbers, Moscow exchange.

How modern.

Beside it, tightly pleated, lay a hundred-ruble note.

Moscow
Kitai Gorod
January 1897

MOSCOW'S STREETS WERE LONG; despite what passed for the warmth of the afternoon, the walk was brutal. Jack asked twice where Irina was taking him; each time she answered with a headshake and what he could interpret as a smile, though her scarf hid the lower half of her face completely.

The streets were frozen into a surface less forgiving than iron. Jack could still see the evidence in their splintery surfaces of how the topmost layer had frozen first and been shattered by hooves. The hard frost had then locked down hard in an irregular, cratered surface that made Jack grateful for the packed snow evening out its surfaces.

"This is a hard place," he said to Irina.

"We are hard people." She said it with pride, so he wondered if by *hard* she meant *strong* or *determined*. Some idiomatic concepts translated directly. Some did not.

The wind bit through his clothing as they walked, stinging his eyes and nose until they dripped fluids that froze against his scarf and his face. Jack found himself huffing in relief as they entered a subway entrance and descended below the reach of the savage cold. He pulled his scarf down. The subway stair was still below freezing, but by comparison it seemed quite comfortable. And when Irina reached out to squeeze his hand as they reached the crowded platform, it might even have been warm.

The crowds encouraged them to ride in silence, and so they did. Jack surrendered his seat to a *babushka* laden with net shopping bags; Irina stood for a woman juggling a baby swaddled until Jack could not even see its nosetip.

The subway car reeked of wet wool and cabbage and indifferently clean Muscovites, overlaid with the pall of coal smoke. Jack had heard that Paris was adopting electric trains; he looked forward to living long enough to see all Europe made cleaner and brighter, not just the Ville Lumiére.

His reverie occupied him until Irina stood, tugging his hand, and he rose to follow as the train lurched into a station. The signs flashed past too quickly for him to sound out the Cyrillic letters, even if he hadn't been muttering apologies and slipping between passengers. The train stopped with a jerk. Jack staggered, but Irina had been ready for it and steadied him. With his other hand he caught the rail and managed to spill out onto the platform with something like dignity.

He and Irina were the only ones getting off here. As he glanced around, she tugged his hand again and then dropped it, striding purposefully towards the stairs.

Jack ran a few steps to keep up with her. Her bootheels clicked more than his did, making him wonder if hers were hobnailed for better traction on the inevitable ice.

Incredibly, when they reached the surface, the cold was worse. The patches of clear sky beyond the buildings opposite told Jack that had emerged near the waterfront, and the wind off the river howled as it cut between buildings—and through his whole body. He fancied he could feel it ripping life and warmth from his very heart, blowing them off like shreds of tattered crepe.

The street was gray and deserted, and the buildings here seemed to be predominantly warehouses and factories.

With a little more available time, Jack managed to work out the words over the door of the factory they approached. It was, he thought, a slaughterhouse or a meat packing plant, and even in the cold air the smell of the stockyards that must lie behind it carried. Jack tried not to think too much of all that animal waste washing down the embankment into a river most of the city still used for drinking water. He hoped they had well-trained sorcerers for treating it.

As she led him up the icy steps to a side door, Jack touched Irina's arm. Slowly, with careful pronunciation, he said, "You're bringing me here to kill me, aren't you?"

She must have followed the sense of it, because she laughed. "Me? No." she said. "But I cannot speak for my friends."

She didn't have a key: the door stood unlocked. As they stepped inside, Jack found himself face-to-cravat with an impressively thewed gentleman who nodded at Irina and frowned at him. —He's with me,— she said, and that seemed to settle it.

Jack's initial impression of the room he stood aside to let them enter was that it was very red. Russians were fond of the color, especially in concert with gold; while the out-sides of their cities were sometimes bleak and gray, and their coats and trousers and dresses black or charcoal to absorb the grime of the streets—but Jack sometimes thought they would enamel *anything*, and their houses and flats were full of enamel and filigree and elaborately etched and faceted ruby glass.

Anything to fight the dark and dreary cold.

Irina did not stay in the red room long. She shed her cold-weather armor, trading coat and baggage to a girl who hung them up behind a counter, and indicated that Jack should do the same. Ten pounds lighter, he followed her down a hallway—clean tile, not the distressing grayness he had envisioned from outside, into a meeting room too large to seem cramped, even though it was desperately crowded.

He recognized some of the people here from various revolutionary cafés in the White City, including Kobalt. As they entered, Irina slid a red-and-black armband from her pocket and twisted it around her upper arm.

Jack, who did not have one, leaned close to her. —I thought you said we weren't going to the labor meeting.—

—This is a different meeting,— she said, as if that explained everything. And maybe it did, although as he watched her pour and sugar tea for both of them, it was hard to contain both his amusement and his disappointment. Was this really a better party than the one at the gallery?

Sipping his tea, his back to the wall, Jack thought *It might as well be the* same *party.* On the other side of a long, cold walk and a subway ride, and with much less interesting things on the walls. As the space filled up and Irina swung in ever-increasing orbits around him, spinning off to greet friends or enemies and eventually returning, he thought he recognized at least a third of the arrivals. There were the Kostov brothers, police informants or not. Nadia, the ginger-haired, layers of shawls over her layers of skirts giving her the appearance of a particularly Bohemian wing chair belonging to a colorblind poet with a mortal terror of drafts. There was Dmitri the counterman, whose art Irina so roundly dismissed. Jack might have been put off by the arrogance of her judgment, were not her own work so manifestly brilliant. That was the other thing about Russian girls, he was finding. They were not shy with their opinions, even the potentially offensive ones.

Jack thought about Sebastien, and from his sheltered position, observed. He was not so accomplished at vanishing into the furniture as a wampyr, though, and when one of Irina's peregrinations left him unaccompanied looked up from his tea glass to find Nadia drawing up beside him, glass beads sparkling amid her tassels and fringe.

"All the boys want Irina," she said, without prologue. "But Irina doesn't want any of the boys. Not for long, anyway. She'll break your heart, English boy."

"Your English is very good," Jack answered. Another thing about growing up in a crèche: one learned which bait to refuse. "Do you think I have a heart to be broken?"

Nadia smiled, turning her back to the wall to stand beside him. They were of a height, and if she was twice his age, she laughed like a young woman. "It turns out, we all do. You just have to find the place where we keep it. Like sorcerers, some of us pull the heart from our chest and invest it elsewhere. You have to find where we hid it."

Jack watched Irina whirl around the room, and was struck by how different she looked from the others present. Laughing, vivacious, mocking. It drew frowns from some of the others—Dmitri, who spoke to her in hushed tones, sternly. Jack said, "She doesn't look as if she's here out of concern for the plight of the laboring class."

"Are you?" He turned to her in surprise. The challenge in her pale eyes was unmistakable.

Jack wondered if he could shock her. "I followed Irina. I thought she was taking me home."

Apparently, blunt honesty was good enough to provoke a laugh out of her. While she was gasping, tears at the corners of her eyes, Jack finished, "But my parents were poor. So poor they had to indenture me because they could not afford to feed me. So yes, I have some sympathy."

That ended Nadia's laughter. She licked her lips, quickly, guiltily, and sipped tea as if to disguise the gesture as thirst. "She probably started coming to these things because Starkad likes revolutionaries."

She was watching to see if he recognized the name. He did not, and likewise did not see any need to dissemble. "Is Starkad the gallery owner?"

Nadia shook her head. "A patron of the arts. We were all in love with him, a little."

Were. But before Jack could pursue that line of inquiry, the door opened again.

Nadia lifted her chin and turned, up on tiptoe to peer through the crowd. Following her gaze, Jack saw narrow shoulders and a dark head poking above the general mass. "Oh, it's Ilya. We can start now."

Apparently, the showing at the gallery had broken up for good. Beside Ilya, Jack saw the gray complexion and thick shoulders of Sergei; Svetlana and Tania were off to his left.

Ilya didn't seem to be making any gestures for attention, but as he moved slowly around the room, Jack could feel the focus of the group settling on him. He had that kind of charisma, the ability to dominate a conversation without saying a word. Even across the meeting hall, Jack could feel it working on him, making him desire Ilya's attention and approval.

When the crowd had silenced enough, it was he who called the meeting to order, speaking too rapidly in Russian for Jack to follow. Jack didn't really need to know what was being said, in its specifics—the hypnotic tones of Ilya's voice, the susurrus of approval that rose to fill each pause, were enough. Jack could feel the excitement sweep over him, as well.

Irina appeared at Jack's elbow, on the other side from Nadia. She'd left her tea glass somewhere, and stood with her arms crossed, fingering the red and black armband that still twisted around her biceps. Her closeness warmed Jack's shoulder. But even when she leaned on him, she never took her eyes off Ilya, whose art she had scorned.

Ilya might not be much of a painter in her estimation, but at this, he was an artist who could hold anyone.

Moscow
Kitai Gorod
May 1903

THE WOMEN WAITED JUST outside. The lady novelist Mrs. Phoebe Smith was prim and pale in a peach summer dress that complemented her blonde hair and skimmed-milk complexion, Abby Irene still regal in her blue evening gown. She hadn't even been back to the hotel, then. It was, Sebastien admitted, good to see them out and together, no matter what the circumstances. Since Jack's death, Phoebe had been too much alone.

As he approached, Sebastien's momentary pang of guilt gave way to admiration. They probably hadn't chosen the colors to complement one another, but then he couldn't be too sure. Especially as since Paris, Abby Irene had taken to dressing Phoebe fashionably, which Phoebe endured with a sort of good-humored tolerance.

It was Phoebe who crossed her arms and frowned most sternly at him. "You lied to us."

Sebastien fell in between them, taking each woman's elbow in one hand and turning them so they walked alongside. The weight of their disapproval warmed him: it was indifference he could not have borne.

"I omitted," he offered, as a sort of compromise. "And only with the best of intentions. And you know I murdered no one. So who was the dead woman, anyway?"

Abby Irene shook her head, which Sebastien understood to mean *outside*. "You don't know?"

"Nor did the good Imperial Inspector tell me. But in any case, he wishes our assistance in solving the crime." Tactfully, Sebastien neglected to specify exactly who he meant, though the detective had not. But then, Phoebe's professional qualifications—while better-known to the general public than those of either Abby Irene or Sebastien— were not so obviously applicable to providing satisfactory resolution to a sudden and bloody homicide.

"I knew the woman whose studio it was," Sebastien admitted. "It was she I meant to visit."

"A courtesan?" Phoebe asked, her voice level and interested. It surprised him that it was Abby Irene who continued to prickle when Sebastien relied on other sources to meet his needs, while Phoebe had adapted to the realities of paying court on a wampyr most easily. Or maybe, he admitted, she was merely still in shock over Jack's death, and her jealousy would flare when she had healed a little.

If she chose to stay with him at all.

"A courtier, yes, but not mine. And when last I knew her, Irina Stephanova had been abandoned by her patron."

He felt the women's reactions in the different ways the muscles of their arms tightened, detected them on changing scents. He bulled on. Some things, if they must be done, were best done at speed. "She and Jack were lovers, though. Six and a half years ago, now."

Abby Irene snapped a glance across Sebastien at Phoebe. Sebastien flattered himself that he was a little more subtle, but he didn't miss the moment of agony that twisted her mouth. No jealousy, that. *Loss.*

None of the pain Sebastien knew she felt as well colored Abby Irene's voice. "So you went to break the news to this namesake of mine?"

"I thought also to throw myself upon her mercy," Sebastien admitted. "But had she not offered, I would have found something at the club."

When Phoebe winced this time, it was for him. In sympathy—which made him in his own turn burn with sympathy for her. For one of the blood, feeding was an intimate experience. A joining, a kind of communion. And it did, Sebastien thought, give the courtesan involved a certain diaphanous link to or control over the wampyr in question. So most of Sebastien's kin chose their courts with care, either out of the pretense or reality of a calculated tolerance for those they dined upon—most of the blood would not admit or demonstrate a fondness for living men—or professionally and with a coldly maintained distance.

If he were rogue, a wampyr might kill, erasing the intimacy with the life. Sebastien knew many who might prefer it that way, but few were willing to risk the retaliatory wrath of humans and of their own kind. Those who did not restrain themselves did not last long, once the evidence began to accrue—and they left a poisoned well for others who chose to coexist more harmoniously with the living.

"So how long since you last dined?" Abby Irene asked in a voice that would have had Sebastien blanching, if he were not blanched already. He had to pause and think, which was never a good sign. If she'd asked, he'd lay odds that Abby Irene knew better than he did.

A cab awaited them in the cracking mud of the street. After helping Abby Irene and Phoebe across, Sebastien handed them up into its chamber.

"Nine days," he admitted.

Phoebe hissed between her teeth. "Take me," she said. "It's been a month. I'll be well."

"You should rely on me to adjudge your wellness—"

Phoebe shrugged. "Oh, yes. You'd starve between us like a donkey between two bales of hay, and then what's a girl to do?"

"Touché," the wampyr said. "It's very hard to argue with such reasoning."

Phoebe smiled and rapped on the carriage roof to start the cab forward. A rattle of reins and the snort of horses came from outside as she began to unbutton the high collar of her dress.

Hiding her scowl, Abby Irene leaned across to draw the curtains. Dawn was indeed coming. Sebastien could smell it.

"Curious," he said, as Phoebe tilted her head back. "The last time I got involved with Irina Stephanova, a murder occurred then also."

Moscow
Kitai Gorod
January 1897

OUTSIDE, THE SHADOWS OF winter evening grew
long quickly. But in her bed below the tall spotless windows
of a top-floor loft converted into an artist's studio, Irina
stretched against Jack's side and pressed her face into the
hollow between his shoulder and his throat. She was warm,
brown against her dingy sheets, her back and flank scattered
with liver-black moles.

She turned to brush her lips against Jack's ear. —You're
not wearing his ring.

Jack's drowsing eyes flew open. He must have jumped
away from her, because abruptly he found himself clinging
to the edge of the cot.

—Excuse me?

—Your wampyr. You're not wearing his ring.

She touched his hand as if by way of illustration, her
breasts swaying gently when she pushed herself up on her
elbows. Her long nipples were liver-black, too, like pieces

of licorice. Jack suddenly had no urge to reach out and cup one, though his fingers still burned with the memory. He pulled his hand away.

—How do you know about that?

—I know all sorts of things,— she teased. —Come back into bed, Jack, before you tip it over.

He edged closer, but stayed wary. It must not have been the response she wanted, because her expression sobered.

—I know because my patron told me— she said. "Here. Look."

She pushed the sheets aside and drew her leg up, turning it aside so he could see the fine-textured scarring along her inner thigh. Just a row of pale dots, shiny against the soft matte texture of her skin. Easy enough to miss, if you weren't looking closely.

Jack bit his lip, choking down envy. Unwarranted envy, in all probability: most wampyrs were not Sebastien.

There was no paler or irritated band on her finger, as there had been on Grigor's. Either she hadn't worn the ring habitually, or she'd had it off her hand long enough for the telltale marks to fade. "You're not wearing a ring either. Who is your patron?" he asked, because that was an appropriate question and he could speak it sanely.

"He goes by Starkad," she said. "Don't worry. He's away from Moscow now. There won't be any trouble."

"There wouldn't have been any chance of trouble if you had let me know you were a courtesan in advance," Jack shot back, but he could see by her expression that what he'd said was too complicated and he'd lost her. He tried again, stretching the limits of his vocabulary. —There would be no trouble if you had told me.

She shrugged, impishly. —But then you wouldn't have come home with me. And I wouldn't have had the chance to meet *your* patron.

Jack stood, leaving the sheets behind, and crouched to find his trousers.

—He's not my patron. He's just a friend.

—❧—

Patron or not, he was unsurprised to find Sebastien waiting in the icy street below, leaning on a silver-shod ebony cane, looking gloriously out of place in his beaver hat and overcoat. A casual inspection would have shown a man of just above average height—five foot eight inches, perhaps: taller than Jack, anyway—with thick black hair that wanted to curl and a swarthy complexion that often concealed his wampyr pallor. An unnecessary muffler wrapped across his face hid the fact that he had no warm breath to mist, but Jack made billows enough for the both of them.

It was only a half-hour after sunset. Sebastien must have come looking for Jack directly upon leaving their apartment.

"What's her name?" Sebastien asked as Jack came up. He presented the perfect picture of nonchalance.

Jack would have chosen to emulate him, but there was no point with somebody who could read your upset on the wind. He closed his eyes briefly, but had to open them again to keep walking due to the hazards of lamp posts and other streetside obstacles. Of course Sebastien knew. If he could follow Jack halfway across the city by scent, he could certainly smell Irina all over Jack's clothes and body.

"Irina Stephanova," Jack said. And then—bitterly, because he trusted Sebastien enough to let him see when he was wounded—added, "She wants to meet you."

"You told her…?"

Jack shook his head. "She knew. It's the only reason she wanted me."

"Somehow," Sebastien said, softly and with a sidelong glance, "I find that very challenging to believe."

Jack stalked ahead.

Sebastien hurried a step or two to catch up. "So," he said, and hesitated. "Do you feel the difference?"

Jack wheeled and stared, the icy winter night searing his cheeks. If Sebastien were human, he would have shot past him a half-step and had to turn, but as it was, he just stopped lightly, his motion—for that moment—preternatural.

"You mean, did she make a man out of me? Oh, *Sebastien*."

Sebastien shrugged and said delicately, "One is curious about experiences one has never had. Evie was my first lover, and she was—no more capable of the human act than I am now. I died a virgin, Jack."

That counted as the sort of confidence one didn't expect from a thousand-year-old friend. Jack thought about it for a minute, while his anger withered and drifted, tugged away as petals by the wind.

"She's somebody else's courtesan," Jack said. "I didn't know until after."

Sebastien might be dead, but it hadn't robbed his face of expressiveness. His hat angled up on his eyebrows. He pulled his muffler down. "That could be problematic. Did she name her patron?"

"Starkad," Jack said.

Sebastien's mouth quirked. "Not a name I know," he admitted. "But he is of course using an alias. And he could be young. I will ask after him at the White Nights."

A cart clattered past at an amble over the frozen ground, two heavy-bodied sorrels who obviously knew their own way bearing along a coat-swaddled bundle of teamsters dozing at the reins. Their red nostrils flared around white columns of breath. Jack squared his shoulders and lifted his chin, letting cold down his collar. "I'm not a child anymore, Sebastien."

Sebastien shook his head. "We are not having this argument in the street, Jack."

"We're having it in English," Jack answered, reasonably. "Who's going to overhear?"

"You cannot provide for me, and I will not—I will not do what was done to you before."

Jack glanced over his shoulder, because the alternative was to kiss Sebastien in the street. He lowered his voice and said, "You damned fool. Have you forgotten you emancipated me? I *want* to provide for you, and I know I can't do it alone. But please—if anything, Sebastien, all today has proven to me is that I do want this, and what happened—"

"You can't say his name, even now."

"*Jaromir.* And it was no more his name than Sebastien is yours. Or John is mine. You bastard, I *want* this."

Sebastien looked at him oddly. "And what if I say I don't?"

"Then I call you a liar." He turned and stalked away, while he still could. He'd wind up back at the apartment— he always did—but at least he could enjoy the satisfaction of a good exit for now.

Except— «Jan» Sebastien called after him, in the language of his childhood. «Jan Vražda. That's your name.»

Jack stopped, hands thrust in his pockets. He considered for a moment, but could not stop himself from turning back. «And what's yours?»

The pause dragged on until the wampyr dropped his eyes, studying the polished tips of his shoes. «It was so long ago. I don't recall.»

Jack waited a long moment before he nodded, giving Sebastien time to think about what he'd said. But no answer nor qualification followed. "I'll be at the apartment if you change your mind," he said, and turned in his icy footprints to wend along the shoveled, snowy banks.

— ❧ —

Sebastien would not have knocked, and so it was not Sebastien's knock that awakened Jack. The pounding on the door made him think of a woman, in fact—it was light and quick and came in flurries, unlike a man's measured, authoritative thumping.

He had a suspicion who it would be before the swinging panel revealed Irina's long face. —How did you know where to find me?

—I asked at the café. Ilya told me which street.

Which didn't answer the question of how Ilya knew, but Jack was certain he'd told one or two people roughly where he was staying. Information traveled in a crowd like that—gossip was one way of keeping each other safe from government agents. And having seen Ilya in action, well—anyone in his coterie would tell him anything he wanted to know. *Who is that young man with Irina?*

Oh, he's the wampyr's courtier—

Irina pushed past him into the flat's narrow kitchen without asking for an invitation. Well, if the sex hadn't been proof she wasn't a wampyr, that would have been.

"You're polite," Jack said.

From the wrinkling of her brow, she didn't miss the sarcasm, even delivered in a foreign tongue. It was the rest of her expression, however, that stopped him. Red eyes, nose swollen—

—What's wrong?— Jack said, already regretting the question even as he was unable to stop himself from asking it.

—Sergei is dead. His body was found in the alley after the meeting today. And the police want to talk to me about it. And you're my...

The last word, he didn't know, but he'd guess from context that it was *alibi*. Jack didn't shut the door. He just stood aside, leaving it open in the obvious expectation that Irina should leave again.

—Christ, is that the other reason you slept with me? So you'd have somebody to cover for you? Who killed Sergei for you?

She recoiled physically, one hand clapped to her mouth, the other clinging to the kitchen counter as she fell back against it. —Jack! I...

She'd been totally unprepared to advocate for herself, and perversely it made him believe her. Being willing to use him to get to Sebastien didn't make her a killer. She stared at him, stricken, until he turned his face away.

"I'm sorry." He shut and locked the door. —I was hurt, and spoke harshly.

—I'm sorry too.— Her chin dropped as she studied her shoes. —I had no one else to go to.

—Sit down,— he said hopelessly. At a time like this, there was only one potential course of action. —I'll make tea.

Moscow
Hotel Bucharest
May 1903

ABBY IRENE SLEPT AT last, and though it was midmorning, Phoebe sat in the sunken living room of their luxurious suite. Surrounded by rich brocade and heavy furniture, she pulled her knees into her chest, her nightgown falling over cushions satiny with embroidery. She looked up at Sebastien, who stood well-back from the window, arms folded, staring out into the brightness of the day. It burned his eyes, blinding, but he found he didn't care much for seeing right now. "If you need to talk—"

He was warm and well, flushed with well-being. It wouldn't do to get too used to feeling thus. He didn't look over his shoulder, but *she* reflected in looking glasses, which this room had aplenty. "What is there to talk about?"

She knew him well enough that the look she shot him was more concerned than offended. She held her tongue, though, which provoked him more than any words.

He said, "If *you* need to talk—"

A thin smile, and finally he turned to face her. In her own intonations, so much more ironic than his, she said, "What is there to talk about?"

He sighed, blinking his eyes to clear the sun-spots that dazzled him. "Jack."

She let her lips pucker in a grimace of discomfort. "Talking won't bring him back."

"Nothing will bring him back," Sebastien agreed. "You know, when—" But the words stuck. He shook his head.

Phoebe's eyebrow rose.

"Before I came to America," he said, "I was tired. The years were heavy. Jack kept me..." ...*alive. Undead. Whatever.* "...in the world."

"And now?"

He shrugged. She stood, and did not come to him.

"Don't you leave me too."

That drew a thin smile. Now, warm, full of her life, he thought he could face the prospect of another fifty years, if that was what it took. What, after all, was fifty years? Abby Irene would never ask such a thing. Abby Irene would never ask a sacrifice of anyone—which, perhaps, was why so few had ever made one for her.

He wanted to ask, *Is that why you chose to come with me? Because I would outlast you?*

But that was too cruel a thing to ask a woman twice-widowed, even if the second loss had been no husband under the church. Sebastien found over the years that he thought more of the heart of man than the house of God; it was more constant in its loyalty and reasons.

"I shall do my best," he said, and knew she knew it was not a promise.

Moscow
Bely Gorod
January 1897

SEBASTIEN WOULD KNOW BEFORE he mounted the stair that Jack had company, who comprised it, and how that company was being entertained. So Jack was anything but surprised when—a little before the sun was due to rise at nine in the morning—the door opened silently and the wampyr stepped in with a restrained bow to the two seated at the tiny square kitchen table where Jack usually ate his cereal alone.

—You must be Irina Stephanova,— Sebastien said. —I am Don Sebastien de Ulloa. I have heard so much about you.

She touched her cheeks as if her complexion hid a flush, looking down. "The police say I make man dead," she said. "You may help me?"

"If I can." Sebastien tugged the door until it latched and came forward lightly across boards that did not creak under his negligible weight. "But you must tell me everything."

He paused between their chairs. Jack scooted to one side to make room for Sebastien to sit. The wampyr slid the stool over from the corner by the counter and perched upon it. Jack thought he liked this kitchen because it was windowless and dim—all the reasons Jack found it depressing. Still, a little sunlight wasn't a matter of unlife and death for Jack as it was for Sebastien.

As he settled down beside Irina, dry and light as a husk, she leaned first away and then towards him. Jack hid his wince at her hopeful expression, the way her hands tightened on the fluted tea cup, so much more English than Russian.

Sebastien shed his coat and gloves on the floor, the muffler still casually looped about his neck. When Irina peeled her fingers off rose-painted china and brushed them across the cold back of his hand, he gave no indication he'd noticed the contact. He just caught her gaze on his and asked, —Where is your patron now, Irina Stephanova?

She looked down. —He left. He did not say where.

—And he did not leave you his ring?

She shook her head, her eyes fixed to the tabletop. She picked up her tea and tried to drink from the empty cup. Just as well it *was* empty, by how her hands shook.

—He took it back before he went.

—And he took back Sergei's, too?

Jack blinked. Of course. He'd assumed Sergei was *Irina's* ex-lover. And perhaps he was: it was easy for courtesans with the same patron to arrange such matters between themselves. It saved on explanations, and at least it kept the jealousies incestuous.

—And that of Grigor, and of Svetlana, and of Ilya—
Irina said. —All of us. We were all his, his court.

—He arranged the gallery show,— Sebastien said, calmly.

Irina nodded. —Lesya, the owner of the gallery, is also
one of his. *Was.* Was also one of his.

Damn. If Sebastien had accepted Jack fully as a member
of his court, Jack thought, *Jack* might have had the experience to be quicker on the uptake. But that was unfair to
Sebastien. Jack was more to blame. He had not been paying
attention to the situation, but only to the girl. He had, in
short, ignored everything about observation that Sebastien
had taught him while distracted by desire.

Irina's expression pulled him back from his thoughts.
It wasn't the befuddlement of an inexperienced courtesan,
but rather the wry acknowledgement of somebody who was
used to wampyrs and their tendency to *know* things. —You
inquired at the club. The Beliye Nochi.

—I learned a little about your patron, too. Starkad, or
Starkardr. What did he tell you when he released you?

Her throat rippled as she swallowed nervously. Jack got
up, taking her cup to bring her back more tea. She seemed
oblivious until he pressed it into her hand again, whereupon
she gave him a grateful nod—but for the way her eyes skipped
off him, he suspected he might as well have been a clockwork
automaton. Actually, something so wonderful might have
actually caught her notice when a boy couldn't, quite.

—He didn't explain things.

—When he left?

—He didn't *explain* things. Ever.

—Typical of the breed,—Jack interjected. Sebastien shot him a look and he smiled, sweet as the jam Irina was stirring into her teacup.

She looked from one of them to the other, possibly startled that Jack would dare to mouth off to a wampyr. But whatever she saw on their faces relaxed her. —He encouraged us to linger in cafés and consort with revolutionaries. He said it made us more interesting. He liked artists, painters, sculptors. He said to me once that men and governments were ephemeral, but the continuity of the world was in its art. I *tried* to be what he wanted.

—He took back his ring,— Sebastien said gently, — because he did not expect to return to Moscow in your lifetime, and such things are never left as heirlooms.

—Oh.— Her mouth worked.

In the parlor, around the corner, light was brightening. Not sunrise yet, but the sky outside those windows would be gray. Jack found himself unsurprised when Sebastien leaned around Irina to glance out the window at the Sorok-sokorov, the forty-times-forty spires of ancient Moscow arrayed against the silver sky.

Well, ancient for Jack. For Sebastien, the next best thing to *born yesterday*.

The wampyr in question leaned back into his chair, his face contented. He spread his hands palm-down on the table and said, —So you did the right thing in coming to me.

She tucked her chin to her chest and shook her head. —They think I killed Sergei.

Sebastien tilted his face at Jack. Jack considered for a moment before shaking his own head emphatically *no*.

On *this*, Sebastien trusted his judgment.

Well, at least it was something. —It will be best if you surrender to the police,— Sebastien said. —Trust Jack and me to investigate for you. We will find the killer.

She shook her head, but Jack could see that she was agreeing.

—How did he die?— Jack asked.

She shrugged. —I didn't hear of any wounds, and Nadia saw the body. He's been unwell for two or three months. I'm not surprised. He hung around with worse revolutionaries than I did. Some who want to *explode* the Tsar's factories.

—He died of hydrargaria,— Sebastien said.

Jack turned and stared at him. Same contentious nose, dark eyes, stern lips, swarthy complexion as always. Same curious, waiting expression. "Mercury poisoning?"

—It had been going on for months,— Sebastien said. — Somebody had been feeding him Chinese red. In quantity.

—Damn,— Irina said. —What a waste. I can barely afford to buy vermilion to *paint* with.

Sebastien smiled—at her flash of spirit rather than the content, Jack thought. He made himself look away.

—So now we ask ourselves what justice is so complete that your patron fled it entirely, or who fears him so much that they waited for his absence to kill his man? What secret is so deep that it was worth killing your fellow courtesan in such a manner that suspicion would inevitably fall on you? Why, in short, are you being framed for this crime?

—Don Sebastien? I don't know. I don't know anything.

—Oh,— he said. —I think it's more likely you don't know what you know. But whatever it is, we'll eventually get to the bottom of this.

He smiled. Jack thought perhaps it was meant to be reassuring. "Jack?" he said.

Jack nodded.

"May I speak with you alone for a moment?"

Jack excused himself to Irina and stood. As he followed Sebastien into the other room, she reached for more tea. He imagined she knew better than to try to eavesdrop on a wampyr.

Sebastien drew him around the corner and lowered his head close to Jack's ear. "It is not comfortable to me for you to consort with revolutionaries."

Jack straightened his spine. "Will you forbid it?"

Sebastien had expressive eyebrows. "You know better than that. You are your own man. But these things— Jack. It's ephemera. Human governments, social contracts, they inevitably fall and are replaced by something else just as terrible. If not more so. It is your nature to exploit and abuse one another. It is not safe to meddle in such things."

Jack nodded. "I know," he said. He hadn't realized until Sebastien attempted to intervene that he was becoming interested in the cause for its own sake, and not merely for Irina. "And it would be inhuman of me to let something awful happen without protest, simply because it is inevitable."

Moscow
Hotel Bucharest
May 1903

ABBY IRENE HAD A particular, aristocratic thinking pose Sebastien thought of as characteristic: left wrist draped over right, shoulders back, chin lifted. When she assumed it, as she did now, lounging behind the breakfast table in their hotel suite, he felt an inner calm steal through him.

Somebody was going to regret ever having picked up a canvas knife.

She fiddled the edge of her juice glass with a fingertip and ignored the dustmop terrier nosing about her feet for breakfast crumbs. Jack's orange cat was nowhere in evidence. The cat and the dog had worked out some détente that only rarely allowed for colocation.

"So what you're implying is that this is not the first time your courtesan was framed for murder."

Sebastien steepled his fingers. "My courtesan...yes. Or no, rather. It does seem likely that the two incidents are related, doesn't it?"

Phoebe was frowning at him. "When you left here, you left her behind. A second time."

Sebastien ducked his chin, accepting the censure. But after a moment, his mulish streak emerged.

"I was only ever here on holiday. Bringing her to Spain would not have been fair. She had a life here," he said. "She had become a successful artist."

With my patronage, but it wasn't his patronage that had made her. Her own talent and diligence had managed that. He had only given her a place to stand—finishing what Starkad had begun.

And he had cut loose from all his court and courtesans after Evie died, when he went to America. Since then he'd had a type—fair and pale, as different from Evie—as different from Irina—as could be.

Jack had kept him from burning, in that terrible time. And now Jack was gone, and somebody else Jack had cared for was in trouble.

"The trouble with having a past is being tethered to it," he said, to watch the women explode with laughter.

"So our first step is to find Irina Stephanova," Abby Irene said. "As it seems likely she may be in danger. Was the murder of Sergei Nikolaevich Vasilievsky ever solved?"

"Oh yes," Sebastien said. "A young man swung for it. And Irina testified at his trial."

He paused, composing himself to say more, but was interrupted by a sharp and steady rapping. Phoebe, still on her feet, crossed the carpets to answer. Before she opened the door, she glanced at Sebastien.

Recognizing their visitor through the panels, he nodded and stood to greet Inspector Dyachenko.

The wiry little man had loosened his muffler and tugged off one mitten, but otherwise looked entirely ready to turn around and march back down the stairs. He was alone.

Mike the terrier ran to the door to investigate, uttering a rapid-fire string of barks. Dyachenko blocked him gently with a shoe. "May I enter?"

Sebastien spared a moment's amusement for the irony of it. One of the blood could enter a hotel room with impunity—whatever mystic authority regulated the restrictions on their power did not consider a lodging to be a dwelling place—but a mortal policeman must wait to be invited.

Human rights, he thought, smiling. "Of course. Would you like some tea?"

"Please." Dyachenko shut the door behind him. His other mitten came off and he stuffed them both into the square patch pocket on his coat. He came up to the dresser to warm his hands before the samovar. It was small of its kind, the coal burner no bigger around than a muskmelon, enamel glistening oil-thick and jewel-deep over chased brass. Phoebe had found it in a secondhand shop, and it kept the Englishwoman and the Bostonian in tea quite nicely.

"We've identified the victim," Dyachenko said, as Sebastien relieved him of his coat and went to fetch another glass and holder. "Olesia Valentinova Sharankova. She was an art dealer and apparently a good friend of Irina Stephanova's. Did you know her?"

The name conjured no face, voice, or scent to Sebastien's awareness. He shook his head, pouring concentrated hot tea into the bottom of the glass and handing it to Dyachenko along with a spoon, to dilute to his taste. Jam and sugar cubes stood on the tray beside the samovar, and Sebastien reasoned that Dyachenko could figure out what to do with them.

He withdrew. "Perhaps Irina made her acquaintance after we parted company."

"Mmm." Dyachenko turned to the ladies as he finished doctoring his glass. "Would either of you care for fresh tea?"

"Thank you," Phoebe said. "Inspector, your English is excellent. May I ask where you studied?"

She held up her glass by the silver handle. He came to relieve her of it. "The University College Dublin."

Abby Irene's eyebrows rose.

Returning the glass to Phoebe, Dyachenko said, "My parents are quite bourgeoisie."

Abby Irene laughed in recognition, and, shaking her head, looked down. Dyachenko smiled at her benevolently. "Ah, I see you know the type."

He set his tea on the table so bits of strawberry seed swirling through cloudy amber fluid caught the lamplight, then settled down behind it. His fingers dipped into his waistcoat pocket and came up pinching something round and silver. He laid it on the table by Abby Irene's hand. "Do you recognize this?"

She made a face and produced a silk handkerchief from her bodice, handling the ring only through it. "I wish you hadn't touched that. You will have disturbed the elements of contagion."

"I am sorry," Dyachenko said. "I am not used to working with sorcerers. But you do know what it is, don't you?"

She studied the stone for a moment, head bent, turning it this way and that. Her expression registered surprise. She handed the handkerchief and the ring wordlessly to Phoebe, who repeated the performance almost identically.

"It's a wampyr courtesan's ring," Abby Irene said. "But that's not all."

Abby Irene turned her hand to display the flat silver band bezel-set with a red trillion-cut garnet that decorated her own finger. Phoebe lifted Dyachenko's ring beside it. They were superficially identical, but the new band was larger and broader, and the stone set in it was oblong in shape and a brilliant, saturated violet-blue.

"Sapphire?" Sebastien hazarded. That had been the stone of preference of one of his own offspring, Epaphras Bull, dead now in Boston in Sebastien's stead—but Epaphras had used a cloudy cat's-eye stone, not this pellucid azure.

"Close." Phoebe rotated the ring and the stone's color faded to limpid clarity, as if by magic.

"*Water* sapphire," Sebastien corrected himself.

"Dichroite," Dyachenko said.

Abby Irene nodded. "Also called *iolite*. It's usually from Sweden or Connecticut, and notable because it functions as a natural polarizing filter. It has any number of thaumaturgic properties and uses, including the ability to increase one's faith. Magi used to trade small fortunes for a good quality lens in the old days. Supposedly the Vikings used it to determine the position of the sun on overcast days, and certainly slips have been recovered from barrows." Her lashes fell across her eyes as she glanced down with a self-conscious smile. "According to some hedge-workers and witches, it's supposed to serve as a protective talisman for women named *Irene*."

"It wasn't on Miss Sharankova's hand," Sebastien said. "*That*, I would have noticed."

"In fact, it's not her ring," Dyachenko said. "It's too big—sized for a man's hand, I'd say, or a large woman's. But it was in her pocket when she died."

"Vikings?" Sebastien said.

Abby Irene lowered her hand and nodded. "Is that significant?"

"I don't know." He folded his arms across his body. "But Irina's original patron was Scandinavian."

"Interesting," said Dyachenko. "Is he in town?"

"I don't know that either," Sebastien said. "But once the sun is down, I can find out for you."

The police inspector smiled like a Pulcinella. "Doctor Garrett, in the interim, would you be so kind as to accompany me?"

"It should be my pleasure." She retrieved the ring from Phoebe as she stood, her indigo silk dressing gown whispering against the wooden chair. "Just allow me a moment to change into morning clothes. You will wish me to examine the body."

"Of course," said Dyachenko, reaching for his tea glass at last. "Mrs. Smith, I am sorry to rob you of your companionship—"

"That's quite all right," Phoebe said with a twinkle. "I am going to be quite busy locating Miss Belotserkovskaya. Since if she is not responsible for the murder, she is no doubt in danger of her life."

"We have men on that," Dyachenko said, nonplussed.

Phoebe smiled. "Sir. No doubt you do."

Moscow
Bely Gorod
January 1897

—TELL ME EVERYTHING YOU know about Starkad,— Sebastien said, taking Irina's hand. She flinched from the chill, but only with discomfort, not the startled horror of one who had never experienced it before. In short, she showed every sign of being—as she presented herself— an experienced courtesan.

Jack settled back in the chair opposite the divan upon which wampyr and girl coexisted, pretending he felt no trace of jealousy. That skill too, was a mark of the experienced courtesan, and one he had a certain amount of practice in. Not that he ever bothered to lie to Sebastien about his jealousy—it would be pointless dissembling, when Sebastien could smell it on him. But he had too much pride to allow his emotions to humiliate him.

Before strangers, anyway.

Irina seemed to be having a hard time formulating her thoughts, or maybe she was still struggling with the shock of Sergei's death. In any case, it was almost half a minute before she withdrew her hand from Sebastien's meant-to-be-comforting grasp and raised her eyes from the floor.

She said, —He's tall. Not like you. Very tall, broad shoulders, white hair and a red beard like a Finn. An accent I never could identify. He dresses like a laborer sometimes. Sometimes in good clothes, but carelessly. He does not play favorites among his courtesans. We do not live with him. He provides for us all the same. Not like you and Jack.

—Jack is not my courtesan,— Sebastien said. —He is my...friend.

Bastard, Jack thought through a pinned-on smile. When Irina gave him a questioning glance, he only forced it wider.

—The blood do not have friends.

Sebastien shrugged. —When you are as old as I am, you have whatever you want. Forgive me if I speak plainly.

Despite everything, the archness of his tone made Jack feel like applauding him. The irony wasn't lost on Irina, either, by the look she gave him.

Sebastien, Jack had the experience to know, did not care to be manipulated. He sat back calmly and said, —I gather Starkad pretty much left you to your own devices.

—He took an interest in my art.

The way she said it, defensively, with the emphasis on the word *my*, told Jack something he should have noticed at the gallery. If Starkad took an interest in Irina's art, it was not a special interest, no matter what she told herself. Of course a wampyr would find willing courtiers among a city's artists—Bohemian, penniless, fond of provoking outrage. But it sounded like Starkad had a closer connection— as if he enjoyed the artists for their own sake.

—Did he frequent any of the underground clubs here in Moscow?

—Not that I know.

From Sebastien's frown, it jibed with what he'd learned from his own contacts there. Jack imagined he'd been hoping for more.

—Do you know any of his other names?

Irina shook her head. —You said Starkardr. That was more than I ever heard.

Sebastien inclined his head. —No one seems to have met him. One or two had heard the name.

Irina grimaced and fumbled in her pockets. —Before you ask, I do not know where he has gone or why he disappeared, either.

—Hmph.— Sebastien sat back, arms folded, his forelock fallen across his eyes. —Most unsatisfactory, Irina Stephanova.

—You're telling me.

If Sebastien breathed, he would have sighed. —What was Sergei to you?

Irina lit a cigarette. —Not so much as he wished to be.

Moscow
Police Palace, Kremlin
May 1903

ANOTHER WOMAN MIGHT HAVE wondered *silently* how it was that the Russian Empire failed to employ some regional equivalent of the Zaubererdetektiv or Crown Investigator, when one of the world's finest universities for sorcerers lay in the garden city of Kyiv. While the Ukraine was not exactly an Imperial possession, that was more a matter of courtesy and title than any lack of tribute paid the Tsar.

But Lady Abigail Irene Garrett, Th.D., had not arrived at her current station in life—doctored, defrocked, deported—by failing to ask such questions as they occurred. So as Dyachenko opened the incongruously beautiful enameled door at the top of the stone steps leading to the police morgue, she rested one hand on the crimson-and-gilt double-headed eagle and paused. Two steps along a descent illuminated by watery electric lights, he turned and glanced back.

A breath of cool air pressed her face, relieving the heat of a day already promising to grow oppressive.

"It was a dungeon first," he said, apparently mistaking her hesitation for confusion or curiosity. "And then it was a wine cellar."

Garrett let one fingertip rub lightly at the eagle's toe, hitching up the blue velvet carpetbag that held her sorcerer's tools in the other. "Inspector Dyachenko, how is it that the Imperial Police have failed to employ forensic sorcerers of their own?"

"We had them." His mouth quirked, fingers curving as he beckoned her to follow. Even when he turned away, she had no difficulty understanding his words, his voice amplified by reflection off all that stone. "But after the Imperial Sorcerers united with democratic revolutionaries to overthrow Ivana III in 1726, it was disbanded, and since then the Imperial family of Mother Russia has…formally discouraged professional organizations for sorcerers. We have hedge-witches, of course, and they have their covens. But those are technically illegal. The University is tolerated, both due to its history and on a technicality—while Ukraine is an Imperial protectorate, legally it has its own parliament and Duke—but you will not find any sorcerer's unions in Moscow or Pavelgrad. I suspect if Ivana had not been a sorceress herself, the entire profession would have been burned out."

"I wonder how I missed that bit of history," Garrett said. Although now that he explained it, the information evoked a familiar tickle in her head. As if she had once been aware of that, in her university days, and it had drifted to that deep quiet place where unrecalled knowledge eventually sedimented.

She wondered if Dyachenko's half-glance over his shoulder was because he abruptly recollected her own recent revolutionary past, and determined not to raise it unless he did.

Thankfully, he held his peace on that matter. He just tipped his ears from one shoulder to the other in a curious sort of shrug and answered her question as if it had been something other than rhetorical. "More pressing concerns?"

She laughed, surprised by how bright and resonant it sounded in the confined space. And unsurprised by the startled glare of the morgue attendant as they came through another, less elaborate door at the bottom of the stairs and into a dim, cool space that smelled of formaldehyde, rose-scented cleanser, and layers of decay. Garrett breathed shallowly, through her open mouth, but that only meant she *tasted* it instead.

Catching Dyachenko's frown, the morgue attendant looked down quickly again. He was a man of average height, thin for his frame, his pin-striped shirtsleeves rolled up and gartered like a banker's. His black bowtie and spectacles only added to the impression of clerical efficiency. He said something in Russian too thick and fast for Garrett to follow, and to which Dyachenko nodded and responded in the affirmative.

He signed them in, and Garrett caught her own name. She also knew the Cyrillic alphabet well enough to recognize its outline when Dyachenko wrote it down.

When they passed through another door into a reeking corridor, the floors of stone so smoothed by centuries of feet they seemed almost sculptured, Dyachenko translated for her. "He was apologizing that the surgeon had not yet been in to perform the postmortem." His shrug indicated that this was usual.

"Is there an honorarium?" Garrett asked, suspecting that such things might be usual here, as they were in New Amsterdam—more so than London or Berlin. It was all about the culture of the place.

"Government employees inevitably consider themselves undercompensated," Dyachenko said. "However, I imagine the delay can only serve your purposes, Crown Investigator."

"Please," Garrett said, surprised by the pang her lost title still sent through her. "Doctor Garrett will suffice."

"I am sorry, Doctor Garrett." Dyachenko paused before a much more modern gray metal door hung counterweighted on swinging hinges. Like all the others along this corridor, it was marked with a number and a letter. "I did not mean to raise uncomfortable memories."

He glanced at her. It was her turn to shrug. A year before, she might have taken him on, but today she was reasonably sure that his blunder had indeed been inadvertent, and besides she was too tired to refight battles she'd already lost.

"It will be cleaner for me to work with an undisturbed corpse," she agreed, and watched his sigh of relief raise his chest and drop it. "Come, let us interview the victim, then."

He straight-armed the door and led her through.

Sharankova's body lay on a marble slab—*like pastry*, Garrett thought, inevitably—with an oiled sheet drawn over her. The slab was supported by a modern chromed steel armature, the tubes forming a number of cubbies and shelves on which her personal effects had been stored. Garrett could just barely puzzle out the labels on the butcher's-paper packages. Clothes, shoes, contents of her pockets—minus the silver ring, of course, though by Garrett's assessment of Dyachenko, she would bet there was a receipt for it.

The dead woman had not been carrying a handbag, which made Garrett wonder what had become of it, or if she had had one at all. Surely some women managed without, though it seemed to Garrett a foreign way of life.

Sharankova's dark hair, blood-clotted into stiff antennae, protruded from under her shroud. There were three other slabs in the room, of which two were occupied. Garrett selected the fourth as a resting place for her carpet bag and set it there. When she turned back to the dead woman, she held a glass rod in one hand, a piece of rabbit fur sewn to a silk backing in the other. "Do you have the murder weapon?"

Dyachenko produced it from the shelves under Sharankova's corpse. He'd taken the precaution of wrapping it in a layer of silk before sliding it into an oiled-paper evidence envelope. Garrett was grateful for his foresight: not every mundane investigator understood the forensic process even that well.

"You'll want the gloves," he said, offering her a white silk pair.

She smiled and produced her own. "You don't use those to avoid leaving thaumaturgical residue." The state of the ring he'd handed her was proof enough of that.

"Fingerprints," he said. "Did you know that no two people have the same pattern of spirals on their fingers? And skin oil left behind when a killer handles something can leave residue in the shape of those whorls. We wear the gloves to protect that evidence." He grinned, delighted to share his trade secrets with a fellow professional, and Garrett felt a sharp and sudden pang. "You have a labyrinth on your fingertips."

Garrett paused before drawing the glove onto her left hand, turning the palm up to the electric lights to see how their sheen revealed the presence of minute ridges and valleys in her skin.

"Did you get anything off this one?"

"A clear thumbprint and partials of three left fingers."

"So your killer is left-handed."

He made that funny shrug again. "It would seem. Or at the very least, someone handled the knife left-handed. It could have been Irina Stephanova, though—even if she was not the killer, one would expect her fingerprints to be on a tool found in her studio. Although it would be more likely that those would be smudged, and these were quite clear, laid over older unusable prints."

"Well, maybe I can help to tell you who the prints belong to," Garrett said. "First, though, I'm going to look for trace evidence on the body. The principle of contagion tells us that any time two things come into contact, each leaves an influence on the aura of the other."

Dyachenko rocked back in his down-at-the-heels boots, clapping silk-clad hands together. "We call it the principle of transference. The idea is that anybody who passes through a location takes something and leaves something behind, and if you can find those things, you can prove that the person in question was present at the scene."

Garrett cocked her head at him.

He winked. "The Imperial Police are very good at murder, Doctor Garrett."

"Yes," she said. "I see."

She unwrapped the blood-caked canvas knife, and laid the triangular tool down atop its wrappings on the empty bench. While Dyachenko stood nearby, arms folded, carefully out of the way, she sprinkled a circle of salt around it and spoke a few focusing words in Latin. She rubbed the glass rod with the rabbit fur, charging it, and touched the tip to the handle of the canvas knife where the victim's blood had smudged it.

"A violent event leaves a stronger thaumaturgical impression," she said. "Almost an imprint. It should override other uses to which the tool has been put."

"I see," said Dyachenko. "So if I use my pocket knife to trim my nails every week for thirty years, and then I stab my brother with it—"

"The stabbing wins," she agreed. "In terms of the aura of the piece. We theorize that this is because we live in a solipsistic world, and intention is paramount."

She had, she noticed, fallen easily into treating him as a colleague. It made sense that the Russians would have developed procedures and sciences the West had not, having removed the forensic option from their investigative process. It would be interesting to see which tactic was more effective.

Garrett waited a moment while the rod attracted wisps of residue from the murder weapon. Carefully holding it elevated—like a sorcerer in a motion picture—she turned back to the slab that held Olesia Valentinova Sharankova's mortal remains. "Would you uncover the victim, please, Detective?"

With gentle precision, accordioning the sheet down in twelve-inch sections, he obeyed. Sarankova lay nude along the slab, eyes clouded and staring. The gummy blackened crimson had not been washed from her throat or hands, and Garrett could imagine how she had clutched at the canvas knife protruding from her throat after the killer stabbed her, trying to deny the inevitable and keep the slick-sticky hot blood within. Garrett wondered if she had come to the understanding that there was no stopping this, or if she had died still fighting.

"We've been over her with tweezers and soft brushes," Dyachenko said. "We collected some fiber and dust, some animal hair—she had a cat. Once we have finished with her, I will put some pressure on the coroner to dissect."

Garrett did not glance over. She could not afford the break in her concentration now. After a moment, Dyachenko seemed to come to an understanding of that, because he shut his mouth and backed away.

Garrett balanced the rod across her fingers and moved it over every inch of Sharankova's skin, starting with the soles of her feet. It showed no response until Garrett approached the neck, when it swung to indicate the gummed slice of the wound. No surprises there, and after bending to inspect the red edges more closely, Garrett moved on.

When it swung again, it was to point to Sharankova's mouth. A superficial inspection revealed only bruised lips, with no sign of foreign material. Garrett looked up to find Dyachenko watching intently, the tip of his tongue protruding in concentration.

"How's her rigor?" Garrett asked.

Dyachenko didn't take his eyes from the dip and shiver of the wand-tip. "You're dowsing for evidence."

Garrett smiled. "It works. Can you get her jaw open for me?"

"I can try. Her arms were already in cadaveric spasm when your—friend found her, which indicates to me that she put up a fight, because rigor is delayed in cases of exsanguination or hemorrhage, but accelerated when there has been extreme muscular exertion. Unfortunately, there was no damning trace evidence clutched in her deathgrip."

"There never is, when it would be convenient."

Dyachenko snorted. He let his hands hover beside Sharankova's cheeks, frowning down at the dead woman. "But this is the second day. Odds are very good that rigor is fully developed."

He touched her cheeks, ran a thumb across her lower lip, and grimaced. "Her jaw is locked, Doctor Garrett. I think I can get the lips apart, but it would take a stronger man than I to open this mouth."

"Lips, then," she said.

"And then I'll fetch the diener. He can help me break the rigor on her jaw, and we'll see if there's anything in there," said Dyachenko.

She watched him wedge his thumbs into the cold mouth and pull, grimacing with effort or distaste. It took force to part her lips, but once it was done, they opened loosely, flaccidly, revealing the pink-stained valleys between her teeth. Garrett leaned forward over the body beside him, their heads almost touching. Garrett's glass rod dipped gently to tap the dead woman's tooth enamel, emitting a soft clink. The inside of Sharankova's lips revealed cuts and abrasions, marks from where they had been jammed against her teeth by the pressure of—perhaps—a hand.

Garrett looked up at Dyachenko. "I can't be sure until we see inside, but I suspect that not all that blood is her own."

"She got a piece of him," Dyachenko said. "That's the American term, isn't it?"

Garrett smiled. "I think she did. Somewhere, somebody has a set of bite marks."

Dyachenko patted the dead woman's blood-stiff hair. "And it's not even my birthday."

Garrett huffed, but in truth she was well-satisfied. "Hand me the ring, would you? We're just going to make absolutely certain it wasn't hers before we proceed with that line of investigation."

It proved not to be, which surprised no one.

Moscow
Hotel Bucharest
January 1897

"YOU'LL STAY WITH US," Jack said, trying to sound as if it were already settled. "Under Sebastien's protection."

Irina looked up at him, startled, her bony fingers caged loosely around her fourth cup of tea. The ruins of a meal of blini, sour cream, pickled beets, and smoked fish lay scattered across the table between them. Sebastien lounged against the wall beside the kitchen window: if this were a Russian flat inhabited by actual Russians, it would be nailed shut against the winter, but Sebastien preferred the option of a quick egress.

Jack supposed enough hasty exits, over the centuries, inured one to the necessity of planning for them.

"But my work—" She shook her head. "Your flat is too small. I cannot bring my canvases here. And where would I sleep?"

Jack gave her a look up through his lashes to make her laugh. It worked, and when she was done she spread her hands in acknowledgement that he had scored.

But her surrender was only partial. "I need my studio."

—Surely,— Sebastien interjected, —you can spare the work of a few days in order to protect your life.

She shook her head. —I have a commission. They are not so common.

Sebastien's eyebrows rose. He glanced at Jack, and Jack nodded. Yes, all things considered, Irina was a better than average young artist.

—Then I shall become your patron now,— Sebastien said. —And Jack and I shall come and stay with you until the commission is completed. And Sergei's murderer is caught.

It seemed as if Irina would argue, but Sebastien leaned forward and folded his arms in a gesture that could not have said *Try me* more plainly if he'd written it on the wall in chalk, and she subsided.

"I must hang paper over the windows," she said.

Sebastien smiled. —We'll see to it tonight. In the meantime, if you are sufficiently refreshed, if I may trouble you for a small favor, my dear?

Irina obviously had no doubt what he intended. Her fingertips crept to her collar. Sebastien nodded.

"Sure," she said, as if she did not trust her voice to say more.

Silently, stiffly, Jack got up to clear the dishes.

—⁂—

Later, while Irina napped on the divan and Jack sat pretending to be engaged in a week-old French newspaper, Sebastien came to him. He perched on a kitchen stool and leaned forward, waiting until Jack collected his temper enough to acknowledge his presence.

"She's, what, three years older than I am?"

"I didn't raise her," Sebastien said. "You're more to me than *dinner*, Jack."

The urge to slap him wasn't doing anybody any good. Jack took it out on the paper instead, crumpling pages in both fists and smearing his palms with dingy ink. This seemed like a good time to change the subject decisively. "So *is* Irina the target, or is it Starkad? Or was it something Sergei actually did himself that got him into trouble?"

"If it was," Sebastien said, "it was something he did to somebody who knows enough about the blood to frame his nestmate."

It wasn't a polite term, which was unlike Sebastien in the extreme. While Jack was still blinking at him, he continued, "I'm uneasy about this Starkad character. What Irina said about her patron is all *anybody* knows about him. Or at least, all they're willing to admit knowing. He exists, he's been using that same name for as long as anyone recollects, he doesn't interact with the society of blood *or* the society of men. I didn't manage to speak to any of the blood who have ever met him, but several of them have heard of a courtesan who used to be Starkad's, and was abandoned before being adopted by another patron."

Jack refolded the paper more neatly, a delaying tactic while he thought. "So this is a pattern for him."

Sebastien nodded. Beneath the taut, dehydrated lines of his flesh, Jack fancied he could see the bones of the young man Sebastien had been. If he ever kept himself fatted on blood, anyone would be able to see that he appeared no older than Jack—no older, and yet he was well-embarked upon his second millennium. The drawn cheeks of hunger imparted a certain authority.

"The afternoon looks like snow," he said. "The barometer is falling. I'll visit the Imperial Police and offer my services as Don Sebastien." The wampyr smiled, and suddenly did not look young at all. "Maybe I'll learn something."

"I'm coming with you," Jack said.

Sebastien lifted his chin stubbornly. "And leave Irina without a guardian?

Moscow
Kitai Gorod
May 1903

THE LONG, STIFLING, JEWEL-BRIGHT days of a Moscow summer made it a seasonal destination for the blood—they descended upon the city in the winter, when the nights were long and the clubs—both underground and above—became gathering places for bored and restive mortals in search of romance, adventure, or just an evening's distraction. The underground clubs were harder to find and harder to gain admission to, but it was in the best interests of the blood to assure that there were means.

Travelers must eat.

In summer, while the lovely old city filled up with mortal holiday-makers, the blood abandoned it for the soft nights of more temperate climes or the sultry and unrepentant tropics. Some took their courts along, but more trusted to Providence or preparation to see to their needs. Which meant an embarrassment of resources for any wampyr left behind—if it also meant limited hours in which to exploit them all.

One element of the secret to Sebastien's long and storied life was his avoidance of conflict, or even the appearance of impropriety. An element of that was respecting the property rights of others. But there were always the would-be courtiers and those whose patrons had moved on, leaving them without rings or affiliation. And they sought out the companionship and community of others like themselves in havens old as the blood.

In the sweet gloaming of a summer evening, Beliye Nochi was such a place.

Sebastien paused amid the spires of the converted eighteenth century Kitai Gorod church housing the underground club and set his back to the central and largest onion-dome to admire the view. The walls were a dull gold that faded to beige in the dusk, and over his head the wall-tops below the brick-hued domes were patterned in intricate mosaics of turquoise, gilt, and ivory. The groin-vaulted roof over the nave would have made a tricky traverse for a living man, but Sebastien floated across it like a shadow, light and quick.

He entered the club through a door cut into one of the smaller towers, lifting off his hat as he came within the embrace of the building. This entrance, though reserved for the blood, lay unguarded. No merely human dexterity would have attained it, and no merely human strength been sufficient to shift it. The door lead through a lightlock to a short, sunproofed spiral stairwell, where translucent windows protected any of Sebastien's blood-kin who might come this far in daylight or who might be caught short in the city, far from other shade.

In silence he descended, where human feet had echoed.

He emerged through a lattice door into the nave of the church-that-was, to find Phoebe in a little gray dress, ensconced upon a little gray chair, waiting at the bottom for him. A rather large, bored-looking courtesan had settled next to her, wearing a ring set with a square-cut diamond and a pleasant expression. He bowed to Sebastien; Sebastien nodded back and then bowed in his own turn to the lady.

She accepted his hand and let him draw her to her feet, though she hardly needed the assistance. Her touch was as light on his fingers as a wampyr's. "Abby Irene didn't choose that dress."

She gave the soft sensible skirts a shake, so they fell into deep pleats around her body. "The dress stands up to dirt," she said, primly, and took his arm to lead him out into the main room of the club. Belliye Noche boasted other spaces in addition to this grand one—there were coatrooms and a conversation area in the old entryway, and the chancel had become a sitting room—but the former nave was both spectacular and comfortable. The windows had been dimmed inside with translucent glass, and cozy nooks established through the strategic use of Chinese screens and groups of furniture. There were two or three of the blood present, and a half-dozen courtesans and staff, but the old nave was capacious enough to seem barely inhabited even so.

Sebastien allowed Phoebe to guide him. She led him to a niche below the clerestory, the sort of corner where lean shadows loomed in apparent despite of the gaslamps and a velvet chaise collected dust. It was unoccupied: Sebastien would have hated to stumble upon a feeding pair who had withdrawn for some discretion, which was a hazard of public spaces in an underground club. Instead, Phoebe settled onto the wine velvet and patted the chaise to encourage him to join her.

Feeling rather like a summoned housecat, Sebastien obliged. The ancient horsehair stuffing barely compacted under his weight. "Old and dry," he said.

Phoebe patted the couch again, a mistress of willful misinterpretation. "But still serviceable. I found Irina Stephanova."

"How?"

"You know my methods, Watson," she mocked, so Sebastien leaned ostentatiously away from her, and she was forced to add: "Do you really think he's inspired by you?"

"Art always outstrips the reality," Sebastien said. "Phoebe—"

"I am sorry." She made a moue of contrition. "But do you know how rarely I have the advantage on you? I spent the morning inquiring after her in artist's clubs and with her friends, and it turned out some few of them had heard your name, and all of them recognized the ring. That, and the tenor of my questioning, must have served to convince someone of the necessity of informing her of my inquiries. She met me for dinner and has agreed on my assurances to turn herself in."

"To Dyachenko?"

"To you," Phoebe said. "She's waiting for you else-where. She did not wish to be seen, and coming here—would guarantee being seen."

Sebastien took her hand, feeling its warmth, its pulse, the curl of her fingers around his. "You've done well, Phoebe."

She leaned her head against his shoulder. "I know."

He nerved himself—there were things no weight of years made any easier—and lowered his lips to her ear to whisper, "and I am sorry about Jack."

She lifted her head and turned to stare at him. "Don't you dare take responsibility for that."

"Phoebe—"

"Don't," she interrupted, "you dare. I was there, Sebastien, and I know how little it was your fault."

"I would have saved him for you if I could."

"And for him, and for yourself," she said, so agreeably he found himself looking for the trap. Confronted with his attention, she sighed and rolled her eyes. "You act as if this is the first time I've been widowed, Sebastien, and while I am not so accomplished upon it as you are, I know how to do this. And so do you."

He stared, and shrugged, and said, "Touché. Does it hurt less the second time, then?"

"You don't know?"

He had to think about it. And then he said, wearily, "Let us say for the moment that I do not recall."

It was her turn to stare, a strand of her hair—the color of winter butter—straggling across her forehead. A moment only, and then she brushed the hair back into her bun and said, "Yes, well, rather, then. Shall we go and collect Irina Stephanova?"

"Yes," Sebastien said, biting back relief. "Let us do so by all means."

Moscow
Police Palace, Kremlin
January 1897

IMPERIAL POLICE INSPECTOR KOSTOV was a tall man, brown-haired, gray-eyed, thin and dressed like he accepted graft. Sebastien, seated across the desk from him, kept his hands folded and in plain sight.

—I am Don Sebastien de Ulloa,— he said. —Thank you for this meeting, Inspector Kostov. Perhaps my reputation precedes me?

Kostov inclined his head, an attempt at graciousness that his words did not support. —I appreciate your interest in the murder of Sergei Nikolaevich Vasilievsky, but I must inform you that we have the situation well under control.

—It so happens that I have been contracted by an acquaintance of the deceased.— Sebastien let his hands fall apart, a gesture of helplessness. —My client is very interested in finding out who killed her friend.

—Your client is Irina Stephanova Belotserkovskaya?

Sebastien was not surprised that Kostov knew that, and even if he had been he would not have demonstrated it. —You had her followed, of course.

This time, the acknowledgement actually did give the impression of generosity. Self-satisfaction looked good on Inspector Kostov. —We know Irina Stephanova is not guilty of the crime. She has nothing to fear as long as she cooperates with our efforts.

—I'm sure she will,—Sebastien agreed. —You make it sound as if the case were solved already.

Kostov smiled. —It's always sex, revenge, or money, Don Sebastien,— he said. —It's easiest when it's all three. Then they write themselves, you know?

—The case *is* solved?— Sebastien didn't mind pressing for answers, but that wasn't actually what he was doing here. He was pressing for reactions, which was a different art form entirely, and this time he got one.

Kostov stood and gestured mock-graciously to the door, concluding the interview. —Bring your client around tomorrow, Don Sebastien. I can assure you she will not be imprisoned. We will, however, expect her to testify.

—❦—

Sebastien, Jack thought uncharitably, was likely to drag them through every ring shop and jeweler's in Moscow before the night was done. At least they'd be likely to close in an hour or so, but in the meantime there was walking, and cabs, and blank looks. All of them were willing to make rings for a wampyr—Sebastien had obtained a list of friendly gold- and silversmiths from the White Nights— but each one looked *blankly* willing at the mention of a water sapphire.

"Iolite," Jack would say, to an even blanker look, and scattered nods.

"It's rare," they'd say. "But if you have a source of the stones, we can do it."

Until they came to a shop in a blind alley near Sokolniki Park, the awnings already rolled up but the lights still on and the door unbarred. There, the woman behind the counter was small and strong-handed, her hair skinned into a knot on the back of her head. She wore fingerless mitts against the draft through the door, and the creases in her eye-corners were at odds with the transparency of her skin.

She nodded decisively. —Yes, my lord. I can make you a ring. What is your stone?

Jack stood back, arms folded, as Sebastien described Starkad's band. —Can you make me a ring like that one?

The jeweler's face compacted and her fingertips paled on the counter's edge. —Not like that one.— she said. — Somebody else uses that stone. You would need another.

—Red garnet?— Sebastien said. —Trillion cut?

She sighed, and Jack thought it was relief. —Absolutely. For the gentleman?

With the nod of her head she indicated Jack.

Sebastien smiled over at him. —For a lady.

Moscow
Kitai Gorod
May 1903

SEBASTIEN FOLLOWED PHOEBE THROUGH rainy late-night streets, contemplating the inconvenience of it. He would have liked to have a word about perversity with the weather gods who arranged for sky coverage after dark, when no sun needed shrouding and no heat needed breaking and the mud, like some swamp-dwelling monster predating the city built across its back, threatened to swallow everyone.

It was a waste of a good rain.

Phoebe seemed to know where she was going, though, which—given her unfamiliarity with Moscow—told Sebastien she'd planned out this route over the course of the afternoon, and maybe even walked it once or twice. He wondered if she'd already contacted—and perhaps warned—Irina. If she had—well, he trusted Phoebe's judgment. Implicitly, and with tested cause. She would have weighed her options and done what she thought best, and Sebastien would choose to rely on that.

Another way in which he had little in common with his brethren in the blood, come to think of it.

Phoebe's path led them into fashionable streets through which rolled glossy carriages, lanterns burning on each corner, the matched teams of horses tossing wet feather cockades on rain-draggled heads.

"I would have summoned a hansom," Sebastien said.

Phoebe in her turn shrugged, shawl hiked up to her collar, and said, "It's not so far now."

Nor was it. Phoebe paused before a modern block of flats, five stories of pale green façade with wrought-iron balconies, and gestured impatiently for Sebastien. You couldn't argue, exactly, and so Sebastien fell in beside her obediently.

—Flat B3,— Phoebe told the stocky red-faced doorman. —We are expected.

She must have rehearsed the phrase, to say it so smoothly.

He consulted his book, an obvious affectation, and when he had paused with his finger on the page said, — Name, please?

—Mrs. Phoebe Smith and Don Sebastien de Ulloa.

He frowned at them over the tops of rimless spectacles. —The lift is on your right.

It was, along with a slight, blond lift operator who took them to the third floor through the power of eavesdropping, because neither Phoebe nor Sebastien had any need to direct him. The floors scrolled past beyond the filigree cage, each heralded only by a hum and a series of slight bumps—and

Sebastien made up his mind to enjoy the novelty of the experience. It wasn't actually his first ride in a lift, but it was the first in some months. When the operator released his handle and the cage settled at the proper floor with the slightest of rocking motions, Sebastien found himself rather grateful not to have plummeted to his death. *Will wonders never cease?*

"Probably not," Phoebe said, as if she had heard him. She nudged him with one elbow and started forward as the lift operator scrolled the cage door back.

The hallway was tiled in black and white diamonds, very modern and very chic. The rattle of the brass lift cage behind them echoed against hard edges, making Sebastien wish for the carpets and upholstery of a bygone age.

Phoebe, unaffected, paused before the door closest to the lift and raised one small gloved fist to knock there. The scent from beyond the door told Sebastien in advance who had lived there, and he wondered that the police had not already arrived. *Perhaps*, he thought, *the apartment was in some third party's name.*

Olesia Valentinova had lived here, while she had lived, and it seemed striking to him that he had not realized until now where Irina Stephanova might have come for refuge in the aftermath of her friend's death. That she had done so enlightened him on certain matters. He knew now that Olesia *had* been a friend, that Irina knew of her death, that Irina also knew that no-one was likely to come looking here. His sense of smell also told him that Irina was alone in the apartment, and that she had not recently been at work.

"Come in," she said, and stood aside to let him and Phoebe clear the door.

It was a little too fast of a greeting. Sebastien thought he would have liked to have tested his ability to just walk inside, because that might have told him whether or not Olesia Valentinova lived alone, or if there were another presence keeping him from entering he apartment. But what he had would have to do for now.

Once they were inside the kitchen, Irina shut and locked the door behind them. She still wore his ring, he noticed—as he could hardly have failed to—though her jet-black hair was cropped at her jawline now and she wore men's trousers and a un-tucked flannel shirt with the braces rucking the tails up this way and that.

The room was large, for a flat, and furnished with antiques distressed enough to seem comfortable rather than precious. The woman who had lived here had been fond of copper molds shaped like hens and roosters, a few ducks or geese among them. The bright things hung along the moldings. Sebastien was fairly certain they were not of Russian origin.

"Mrs. Smith wouldn't say much," Irina Stephanova said, offering them seats at the dark, scarred table with her gestures. "I take it you don't think I killed anyone?"

"Were you in the room when Olesia Valentinova was killed?" Sebastien felt no need to sit. He chose instead to hover beside the table.

"I found her." Irina shook her head, in dismay or negation. "I found the slashed canvas. I remembered Sergei, and it seemed best to me if I…make myself scarce before whoever did this came back."

"Sergei," Sebastien said. "So you've changed your mind about *his* killer?"

He might not sit, but Phoebe sank down gratefully enough, and Irina across from her. Irina, hands folded on the table before her, nodded. "I never really was sure about Ilya," she admitted. "But the police were so convincing." She shrugged. "Sebastien, where's Jack?"

She must have suspected, by the lift of her chin and the way she was at pains to meet his gaze directly. And it wasn't as if he could lie or temporize. Not to Irina.

"He was killed," Sebastien said. "I am sorry."

Expecting it or not, she rocked with it. Back, and then forward, as if bad news had a kind of momentum. "I am too," she said, her voice thin but determined. "I know what he meant to you."

Beside her, Phoebe was white-knuckled, chin tucked. Grief, Sebastien had reason to know, never got easier, though each individual case of it did fade in time. And in time, one developed strategies.

People still sometimes got inside the armor, though. And whether Jack had developed it during the time he had been indentured, or if it had been native-born in him, like his charisma—insinuating himself into the affections of just about anyone had been Jack Priest's particular gift.

"So you have come to Moscow to tell me this?"

He shook his head. Her English had been improving already when he and Jack left her. He was not surprised to find she had kept it up. Practice was the best cure for monolingualism.

"Not only to find you, anyway. But I thought you should hear it from me. And I seem to have arrived in the nick of time."

"Sebastien," she said, shaking her head. "If I did not know better, I would say you brought death in the folds of your coat. But of course that would be silly."

"Of course," he agreed.

"Mrs. Smith, can I fetch you tea? Lesya wouldn't have minded."

"Tea would be—"

"Lesya," Sebastien said, his head tilting with a memory of six years past. "Olesia Valentinova. Lesya."

Irina nodded. "Of course. It is the common nickname. Why does it suddenly concern you, Sebastien?"

"The gallery owner who hosted your show, when first we met. Lesya. You never said her full name then, and I never met her. But I have—" he let himself smile, slightly, self-deprecating and not so widely as to be out of character for a murder investigator. "—a very good memory for names."

"She was. She was an old friend." Irina Stephanova stood and moved to the counter. Sebastien saw no sign of a samovar, and indeed Irina went to fill the kettle and light the gas stove like any Englishwoman. It charmed him, as did the copper hens, and made him wish he had known this xenophilic Russian gallery owner.

"At the time, you also said she was one of Starkad's courtesans."

Irina nodded. She put her back to the counter, folded her arms, and rubbed her own ring, the trillion garnet flashing in the gaslight. "At the time, you thought it was possible that whoever killed Sergei wanted to get to Starkad."

Sebastien steepled his hands before him. "Do you still think Ilya was behind it?"

"He confessed—"

Sebastien cocked his head at her, and her lips crumpled together like paper.

"No," she said. "I think the Investigator—Kostov—convinced me. I think Sergei's death was a useful excuse for the police to get rid of Ilya before he fomented rebellion. And I know they were eager for all of us, his friends, to give evidence. Dmitri, Svetlana, and me in particular. And of course you know that Sacha and Grigor were the Investigator's sons. I always suspected it was Sacha who put his father onto Ilya. But I don't *know*."

Sebastien tried to bring some life into his face, to make himself seem more compassionate, more warm. More human, if he were being honest with himself. "Would you speak to another Imperial officer? This time, I think, a better one?"

She winced. "There are no better, Sebastien."

"There are always one or two honest men," he argued. "It is the world's tragedy."

She shook her head. "I am sorry I spoke against Ilya, and I do not think he killed Sergei. I think I killed him, because Inspector Kostov wanted the murder solved, and wanted a revolutionary to hang for it. A tidy, *political* solution, that took the heart for revolution out of all of us. And where am I now, and where is Kostov?"

"He is a judge," said a new voice, unheralded by any of the traces of a presence—living or dead—that Sebastien normally relied upon his sense to provide. "And some say in line to be minister of justice. And then he will be dust."

A mortal would not have seen Sebastien move, and there was no drama of overturned tables or broken chairs. Sebastien was simply across the room, before the door that must lead back to the bedrooms, turned to face the hallway. He kept himself between the voice and the women, but far enough from them that he would not harm them incidentally if he had to move.

What stood framed in the doorway was a bony man, pale-haired and strawberry-bearded and livid with the pallor of the hungry undead. He was so tall that Sebastien at first denied the evidence of his own nose, ears, and eyes: surely this could be no elder of the blood, for all his stillness, dryness, and lack of scent. But all those senses supported the impression of immense age in the one Sebastien faced. Now merely tall and broad, in his own age, Starkad had been a giant of a man.

Sebastien eyed him a moment longer, noting the way the linen shirt hung from Starkad's branch-thin limbs, the color and cut of his brown-black burned velvet waistcoat and the weight of the turnip-shaped fob watch whose chain closed it.

He appraised Sebastien for a moment, then cast his blue eyes, water-transparent as the jewels in the rings he gave his courtiers, towards Irina. "So this is what you left me for? Not bad."

Starkad's English accent was exquisite, cultured, and a hundred years or so out of date. Sebastien had no doubt that his Russian would be similar, and perhaps even more archaic.

Irina pressed her hand to her breast, her other one clenched at the wrist, turning her fingers as if to conceal Sebastien's ring. Starkad glided from the hallway, silent as if his steps fell on down and not shoeleather. He had, indeed, the main part of a foot on Sebastien in height, and inches across the shoulders. Such matters mean less among the blood than mortals, but it was still an advantage. And for once, Sebastien could not rely upon the privilege of age to make up the difference.

"Well met, Starkad," he said, and bowed lower than— strictly speaking—he must. "I have heard a great deal about you, and all of it at second hand."

The elder smiled, and with a hand that could not have seemed less negligent, tucked an unfashionably long lock of hair behind his ear.

Sebastien had survived for as long as he had through acclimatization: his grip lay light on the long years, and what they ripped from his grasp he let spin away without too much longing or regret. It let him live in the world, live *with* the world—and his courtesans—in a way most of the blood considered peculiar. But there were other tactics—*as many adaptations as immortals*, Evie had once said, when she kissed him—other ways to move through the world when the world was always moving past you.

And one of those was to become unstuck in time, unglued from human society. Watching Starkad cross the kitchen—slowly, his gestures devoid of threat or nervousness—and knowing what he knew of him, Sebastien blinked with a realization. Starkad was so old that to survive he had come unstuck, not just from human society, but from the timeless society of the blood as well.

Starkad smiled at him, showing the tips of skinned fangs—Sebastien wondered, in that moment, if the display were threat, arousal, or both—and murmured, "I have oft heard you mentioned as well."

His own teeth sharping in his mouth, Sebastien gulped saliva. The meal he'd taken from Phoebe was still fresh and hot in his veins, his flesh juicy with it. He wondered if Starkad could smell it in him. From the way the elder's nostrils flared, Sebastien thought perhaps. If he could scent the blood in Sebastien, he was sharp-set indeed.

Behind Irina, the kettle began to sing. She spun around, every gesture crisp with nervous self-awareness, and pulled it from the burner. With her other hand she killed the flame. As if turning her back on the wampyrs would somehow keep her safe from them, she busied herself with tea and pot.

Phoebe, by contrast, sat very still, her hands folded in the skirts of her dress.

Sebastien refused to be distracted. He squared his shoulders and drew himself up to all his height and what little authority he commanded in this situation, under the customs of his tribe. This lack of status was a sensation that had grown unfamiliar with disuse, and he found he savored it in its novelty. "It seems someone desires your attention, Starkad. Is it only these two of your courtesans who have been murdered, or are there more?"

The elder vampire shrugged, stepping back, and only then did Sebastien realize he had lifted his own chin in order to meet Starkad's water-sapphire eyes. He broke the connection and made himself relax, shoulders down, arms casual. "I have not yet ascertained," he said, softly. He looked over Sebastien's shoulder, to Irina. "I have heard he slashed a painting."

She nodded and did not look up. "It is true. A nude."

The wampyr did not show emotion. He did not frown, or offer any clue at all to what he might be feeling. Sebastien could not even pick it from his scent.

But he nodded, and said reassuringly, "While that cannot be set right, I shall see that, for it, someone pays. They wish you to meet with a police officer?"

She nodded, hands twisting. From the bob of her throat, Sebastien knew she already realized what Starkad's will would be and wished to argue—and that she would no more argue with Starkad than—well, than Sebastien would. The presence of the elder predator was such that it was an act of will for even Sebastien to stand against him.

Evie had been like that sometimes, when the spirit was on her, but even she had not been so old. Sebastien was not at all surprised when Starkad said, "Then speak to the policeman you shall." Starkad ducked his head to smile at Sebastien through his lashes, a coquettish expression for such an ancient face. "Such desecration deserves a response, and if there is an honest policeman in all Moscow, I trust my brother Sebastien would have found him."

Moscow
Bely Gorod
January 1897

"I REMEMBER FIRST TIME I met patron," Irina
said without lifting her head from Jack's shoulder. She'd
changed the sheets. Her skin lay against his, moist and a little adhesive, uncomfortable and alluring. His hand rose to
stroke her hair, tucking it behind one leaf-tender ear-edge.
He wondered if he should mention to her that it seemed a
little...uncultured...to conduct a postmortem of one love
affair while lying in the arms of the replacement.

She seemed immune to his discomfort, or perhaps her
reaction was lost in translation. She told him—he thought,
picking out the sense of what she said from the jumbled
words—that Starkad had found her painting the Moskva
by night in autumn, the lights on the far bank reflecting
streaks across the water. Jack thought he remembered the
painting dimly, having seen it hanging in the gallery before
being distracted by the magnificent flame-colored panels
that dominated her display.

He had come up to her and leaned over her shoulder, but somehow his presence had not made her jump. There was no threat in him, she said, but only a kind of hypnotic calm. He'd complemented the movement of her painting, and suggested that the water, in the dark, reflected a little more crimson.

Upon examination, she had discovered that he was correct. When she turned to thank him, she found him regarding her, she thought then, like a ghost in a mirror. —It is a good thing that you make art,—he'd said. —Art will be around a long time.

She turned to brush her lips across Jack's collarbones and he tried to make himself relax into her embrace. It half-worked, at least until she said, "Do you remember how you met Sebastien?"

Jack made a wheezing noise. It might have been a sigh except where it squeezed past the tightness of his throat.

She was looking for a story like her own, one of high romance, and Jack did not have that to give her. He stretched out beside her and tried not to sound too cruel when he said, "He bought me."

It seemed a long time before she stirred, and longer before she spoke. She laid her head against his shoulder and said, "But he had only the best of intentions."

That she was correct did not make Jack any less irritated with her. It was possible, in fact, that her correctness only served to increase his annoyance. He sat up abruptly, shedding sheets and girl. "Come on," he said, reaching for his trousers. "Let's go find something to eat."

It had been an excuse: he wasn't particularly hungry. So it was a relief when, fifteen minutes later, Sebastien let himself into Irina's studio and announced that he and Irina must present themselves to Inspector Kostov within the hour.

IT WAS A STRANGE thing, walking through Moscow in the company of two mortal women and a prince of the blood as vanishing old as Starkad.

Vanishing was the proper word, too—he was hard to hold in one's attention, except when he chose to dominate it. It was as if he existed in some way sideways to the rest of the world, so that he faded into the backdrop until he asserted his presence. When he spoke, though, a spotlight might have picked him out on the proscenium of some invisible stage, and all around him faded into darkness.

In another thousand years, Sebastien wondered, *will I be like that?*

"You don't associate with the blood," Sebastien said, dropping back to walk beside Starkad.

Starkad paused for a moment as if remembering how before he shrugged, his ash-pale locks breaking over his shoulders. "I did," he said. "Before there were clubs and associations and rules and traditions. Before there were so many expectations."

"All those people are gone."

"Yours too." It wasn't a question.

The acknowledgement, Sebastien could see, cost Starkad an effort. So much work, relating to others, when the silence inside one's own head had become so immense.

Sebastien, half in compassion and half in fellow-feeling, let the conversation lapse, and instead nodded silently and went ahead to flag down a cab.

Less than forty minutes later, he led his little crew into the front doors of the Police Palace and paused before the reception desk. When he identified himself, the desk matron nodded. —Inspector Dyachenko is expecting you. One moment, and a page will guide you in.—

Sebastien knew the way, of course, but he also understood the exigencies of traffic control in a public building. And it was not as if he were short of time. Starkad seemed more a statue than a creature, standing cold and immobile behind the women, who—as if by contrast—moved and breathed and glowed with life. He could have been replaced by white marble with perhaps only a lessening of effect.

The page, when he arrived, was a curly-haired young man in a red-piped navy uniform who said only —Come with me, please,— and —Inspector Dyachenko is in this office here.— before rapping on the doorframe and leaving Sebastien and his companions to their fate. And though in this good light no one could have mistaken Starkad for other than he was, the page made no remark and gave him no more than a second glance. The added stiffness in his spine could even be mistaken for an adolescent's attempt at official dignity.

Before he came up to the door, Sebastien knew that Dyachenko was not alone in his office. He made sure he entered at the vanguard of his little coterie, so he could come around to the chair where she waited and bow over Abby Irene's hand before making the series of introductions necessary. And, if he were truthful with himself, assess the situation for an extra fraction of a second.

Dyachenko's desk was covered in a silk drape Sebastien recognized from the depths of Abby Irene's carpet bag, and on it lay several objects of interest. Starkad's ring, the canvas knife that had protruded from Olesia Valentinova's throat, the note summoning Sebastien to the scene of the crime. Some glass slides sealed with cover slips, which Sebastien presumed held lifted fingerprints. Tiny glassine envelopes that must enfold hair or fibers, or fingernail scrapings. A bloody cotton swab.

Irina's face did interesting things as she entered the office and took in the display of evidence. Phoebe looked like herself, reserved and compassionate. Starkad remained stone, when Sebastien might have expected his hand to flick out at least toward the ring.

By the time Sebastien completed the introductions, though, the elder had marshaled a response. He spoke in English, which was either an unexpected consideration for Abby Irene and Phoebe, or a failure to notice that it might behoove him now to switch. "That is not all Lesya's blood."

Dyachenko had been seeing that Irina and Phoebe were seated, but other than nodding to available chairs, had left Sebastien and Starkad to fend for themselves. He seemed disinterested in the common human habit of enforcing social niceties on wampyrs, which made Sebastien wonder again were he had gained his comfort with Sebastien's tribe. He lifted Starkad's ring with a scrap of ivory silk and handed it to the wampyr.

"We know," he said. "Some of it is from her assailant. Do you recognize it?"

"The ring or the blood, policeman?"

"I know you recognize the ring."

"It is the one I provided to Ilya Ilyich Ulyanov, a painter who was a member of my court. When I closed my court in Moscow, in eighteen hundred and eighty-six, he did not return his ring to me. He told me then it had been stolen. I had no evidence then that he was lying."

"The ring was recovered from the pocket of a more recent murder victim. Please answer my question about the blood."

Starkad closed his eyes and sniffed, delicately, like a parfumier analyzing the notes of an unfamiliar fragrance. Sebastien heard Phoebe holding her breath as he did it, and thought her response unconscious.

Sebastien could identify the presence of the dried blood of two distinct persons in the room. One, he knew by experience to be Olesia Valentinova. The other—

"I am not familiar with the blood of that person," Starkad said, after a pause to consider. "I should like very much to tell you that it has familiar elements, but—"

Dyachenko nodded. "Too bad. And too much to hope for such an easy solution, I suppose. You will provide us with a list of your court in Moscow?"

"I have no court in Moscow," Starkad said. Sebastien watched Irina's face for a reaction, but it might have been carved of the same stone as the wampyr's, albeit in a browner shade.

"But you did," said Phoebe, lacing her fingers together in her lap. "And two of them are dead. A most poetic justice."

Starkad nodded. "Three of them, counting Ilya. My former courtiers, I will gladly provide a list of."

Silently, Dyachenko offered him paper, a clipboard, and a pen, then turned to Irina. "Thank you for coming in, Irina Stephanova. I know this is hard for you. The victim was a friend?"

She nodded.

"And this is not the first time you have been connected with a murder."

"It is not," she said, over the intermittent scratch of Starkad's pen. "I am beginning to take it personally."

Dyachenko reseated himself behind his desk. "That may be a reasonable response," he said. He glanced at Abby Irene. "Doctor Garrett, your forensic findings, if you please?"

She straightened her skirts with a quick, precise gesture, as if preparing to stand, but did not actually rise. Her long-fingered hands grew thinner with every passing year: incrementally, but enough to hurt Sebastien, even so. He thought of Starkad's anger, all directed at the defacement of a painting when a woman lay slashed to death beside it. The loss of something that might endure more than the bare century of a long human life might weigh heavily on an immortal—and aiming one's emotions there did relieve one of the burden of outliving mortal companions. If Starkad chose to surround himself with a court of artists, perhaps that was why: he could fix his affections on their material results and keep his heart intact in ways Sebastien could only imagine. Imagine, and perhaps envy.

"Since you have identified the ring, sir," —she nodded to Starkad— "that answers one question—but raises more. Such as why did the victim have a dead man's missing or stolen ring in her pocket? And why is there no trace of her upon it?"

"No trace?" Phoebe leaned forward, hands braced on her knees.

Abby Irene smiled. "Olesia Valentinova never touched the ring—not with her living hand, nor with her dead one. She left no fingerprints on its surface, and there is no thaumaturgical contagion."

"So the ring was planted," Sebastien said.

"More than that, the ring was planted by the killer," Abby Irene said. "The same hand left traces—thaumaturgical and physical—on both it and on the canvas knife that was used to slash the painting and Olesia Valentinova's throat."

"I see the letter Irina sent me there—" Sebastien said.

Irina glanced at him. "I sent no letter."

Around the room, shoulders squared and chins and eyebrows rose. Only Starkad remained unmoved, which was probably as it should have been.

"I see," said Dyachenko. "So you were lured there in order to discover the body? How intriguing."

"I believe Ilya was framed," Irina volunteered. She glanced at Sebastien. "So why not frame another friend?"

"But one not associated with Starkad, this time?" The detective fanned his fingertips in a quick, reflexive gesture of frustration. "I was hoping we could explore that angle a little further."

"That's not necessarily a lack of connection," Abby Irene said. "After all, they are both of the blood. With the planting of the ring, and the attacks on his court, it begins to appear more and more that the purpose of the attacks is to draw out Starkad."

Judiciously, the blond wampyr nodded. "It would appear so, would it not?"

Dyachenko, though, is on a different trail. "Who do you think framed Ilya Ilyich, Irina?"

She stopped, mouth open, whatever she had been about to say blown back down her throat by his question. Her hands rose and fell, hopelessly, then rose again as if warding off something only she could see. "I—can't say. Inspector."

Dyachenko nodded to Sebastien, which led Sebastien to the realization that he was standing closest to the door. Gently, guiding it so the latch caught almost soundlessly, Sebastien closed it.

"Off the record, Irina," Dyachenko said, while Starkad methodically wrote another name.

She glanced at Starkad—not Sebastien, and Sebastien would have been hard-put to criticize her decision. Besides, the first loyalties were usually the deepest ones.

Starkad nodded without looking up from his task.

"Imperial Inspector Kostov," she said. "If he was not responsible, he knew who was, and he knew of it. He should never have been on the case."

"Kostov is no longer in the department," Dyachenko said.

"I know," Sebastien said. "Starkad mentioned he had become a judge."

Dyachenko's smile thinned. "One of his sons works for me. A lad about your age."

"Grigor?" Irina asked carefully.

"Sacha," Dyachenko said, all competence and calm. "Grigor is an artist, is he not?"

"Grigor is on my list," Starkad said. "And yes. He is a very fine artist. Or he was. His brother—"

"Is a poet," Irina said, just as Dyachenko said, "Is a policeman."

Dyachenko got up from his chair and came around his desk. He opened the door beside Sebastien and leaned out.

—Pyotr,— he said. —Send in Kostov, would you?

Moscow
Bely Gorod
January 1897

JACK HAD INTENDED TO lead Irina back to her loft when Sebastien returned her to him, but she insisted on returning to her habitual haunt—Kobalt, the café where they had met. Named for a pigment named for a goblin, which Jack found appropriate and disturbing in equal measure.

"This is unwise," he said, but she shrugged and swung her handbag in a manner that precluded him enumerating why.

"If you are scared or lazy, you wait at home."

She was not his prisoner. Sebastien was going to kill him, but what else was he supposed to do? Chain her to a steam radiator?

Jack sighed and found his hat.

Inside, it was the usual crowd of revolutionaries, artists, and poseurs—with, Jack thought, a high degree of correspondence between the three categories. Nadia, the young redheaded woman with the cropped hair—quite radical—rushed up to them and said —Irina! Have you heard?

—About Sergei?— She nodded. —I have heard, yes.

—Ilya has been arrested! The police are saying he killed Sergei for you, Irina. Is it true?

The news obviously had the effect on Irina that the girl had been hoping. —Sergei? No, I—why would I want Sergei *killed*?—

Whatever Nadia said, it was too fast and too complicated for Jack to follow, but it was easy enough to understand what Irina was saying. Over and over again, *Nyet, nyet, nyet. That was never my intention.*

He found her hand under the table and squeezed it. She squeezed back, once, but from then on it was as if she had forgotten she had appendages. She just leaned forward, listening, her extremities growing ever colder to his touch. Eventually, she sat back and made a chopping gesture with her hand. —Enough, then. Enough. If Ilya killed him it was not for me.

Nadia looked doubtful, but her frown and whatever might have followed were interrupted by a demanding voice calling her name. She lifted her head and turned. Whoever beckoned must have had a claim on her, because she sighed and stood. —This conversation isn't over.

Judging by the stubborn look gracing Irina's features, she could not have been more wrong.

As Nadia vanished, Jack leaned over to Irina. —I think you're not telling me all the truth about Sergei. It's not just that you were both Starkad's courtiers, is it?

Irina tossed her hair and sighed melodramatically. She looked down, and then sideways, before she said, —The worst kind of men show you the very best time.

Moscow
Police Palace, Kremlin
May 1903

UPON ARRIVING IN HIS superior's office, Sacha Kostov obviously expected something quite different from the panel of inquisition that awaited him. Just within the door, he balked like a nervy horse. Dyachenko slipped a hand inside his elbow and drew him in, and Sebastien shut the door in his wake.

—Officer Kostov,— Dyachenko said, —I order you to remove your jacket and uniform blouse.

The serried colors that rose across Kostov's face left no doubt as to his mortality—pink, then ruddy, then sallow.

—Sir,— he protested under his breath. —There are ladies.

—There are investigators,— Dyachenko replied. —You will disrobe.

—My father will hear of this,— Kostov hissed, his voice cracking on the angry stage-whisper. The glare Kostov directed at Irina and at Starkad could have peeled paint, in particular.

Dyachenko merely nodded, as if accepting the threat at face value, and made a peremptory gesture. —Quickly, please.

Eyes pinned on the floor, Kostov slipped off his jacket and unbuttoned his sleeves. The blouse was some blend that held a press and made a plastic, slithering sound as he shrugged out of it. Sebastien, nose flared, caught no scent of blood, and there were no marks on Kostov's arms, now bared from the biceps down, nor any bulge of bandage beneath his undershirt.

—The rest of it,— Dyachenko said, though now a note of apology crept into his voice.

Kostov raised his chin, but restrained his protests. With one swift movement, he jerked the undershirt up over his head and tossed it to the floor. Kostov's chest and back were reasonably fit, moderately furred, and entirely devoid of the half-moon crescents of human teeth.

"No marks," said Abby Irene, so very gently. —Officer Kostov, you may resume your uniform. I assume you have no objection to providing Inspector Dyachenko with a blood sample?

Kostov's head jerked from one side to the other so hard Sebastien fancied he heard it snap. —None whatsoever,— he said through clenched teeth. —Do you have a particular location in mind?

—I should think a finger prick will suffice.

Abby Irene drew a lancet and a slide from her bag and handed them to Dyachenko. Grimly, his mouth stubbornly immobile, Kostov held out his right hand, and Dyachenko pricked it and took a smear. The scent worked in Sebastien's nostrils. Across the small office, Starkad shook his head *no*, and Sebastien knew before Abby Irene pulled out her wand what the answer would be.

Dyachenko seemed to accept the wampyrs' determination without her confirmation, at least temporarily. —The purpose of this little exercise, Officer Kostov, was to clear you in the murder of Olesia Valentinova Sharankova. We have reason to believe that whoever killed her wished revenge upon her patron, the wampyr Starkad, and it has come to light that your brother Grigor was also his courtier. This served as a link between you and the victim that you failed to disclose in the course of the investigation.

Buttoning his uniform blouse, flipping flat his collar, Kostov grimaced—but some of the offended stiffness dropped out of his spine. —I understand, Inspector.

—The intent was not to humiliate you, Officer, but to clear your name before all concerned.

Kostov's nod could not have been stiffer if a puppeteer had jerked a stick to cause it. —It is not,— he said, at great length, while shooting his cuffs just so, —that I was never envious of my brother, you understand. Because I was envious, of his talent, of the attention it garnered him.

Carefully, Kostov did not glance at Starkad. Starkad had no such qualms, and calmly gazed upon the officer, not even troubling himself to hood his glances.

—I understand that it is difficult to admit such feelings,— said Dyachenko.

Kostov swallowed. —I did not kill anyone.

—No,— said Starkad. —I do not believe that you did.

Moscow
Kitai Gorod
January 1897

WHEN JACK OPENED THE door on Irina, she was
not weeping. From the creases across her forehead and the
pinch at the corner of her eyes, it was only by an act of
will; he could imagine the tears frozen across her cold-red
cheeks. What color would that be? The same Chinese red
that had been the slow death of Sergei Nikolaevich? Or
something with a bluer tone?

You do not have an artist's eye, Jack Priest. —Come
in,— he said. —You look upset.

It was midafternoon; Sebastien was knitting socks in
the darkened parlor and Jack had just pulled cheese and
butter from the icebox for tea. The kettle was steaming,
about to boil, and Irina nodded tightly as she shut the door
behind herself, sliding the bolt reflexively.

Jack reached to touch her shoulder through the coat.
She leaned into it for a second, cold wool exhaling the icy
air of the street around the pressure of his fingers, and then

she shook him off and moved past, into the bright, inviting kitchen. He'd drawn the shades for Sebastien's sake, but it was no great hardship to keep the lamps burning through the day in this cold.

"Please," Jack said dryly as she pulled out a chair. "Sit, Irina."

Her mouth quirked. "Is bad day," she said. "I come from Kostov again, you know?"

He knew. The kettle whistled; he went to warm the pot and pour. There was already sugar on the table, and Jack worked in silence until he could set the chipped porcelain teapot, painted with violets, beside it. Irina said nothing, seeming grateful for the silence. She shed her coat and gloves and scarf over the back of the chair, then rested her chin on her hands.

Jack poured for her, as she seemed disinclined to reach for the pot, but once the cup was in her hands she cradled it close. "Is warm," she said. "Is good." And lowered her face over the steam as Sebastien came into the room, trailing a wreath of variegated merino.

—Ilya?— he asked, in cool tones that somehow conveyed understanding and empaty.

—Kostov,— she answered, hopelessly. —He knew the answers he wanted.

Sebastien sat down beside her. —And you gave them to him.

She nodded, painfully, over her tea. —I didn't know how not to.

Sebastien put a hand on her shoulder. Jack, watching, reached across and did the same thing on the other side. There wasn't much to say that wouldn't be useless. Jack had learned young that there were moments in life best acknowledged by quiet solidarity.

—Some revolutionary I am,— she said, bitterly punctuating the silence.

—Live to fight another day,— Jack answered.

Sebastien shifted. Jack gave him a look, forestalling the inevitable cynical comment—for today, at least. Sebastien's long view was the last thing Irina needed now.

Minutes went by before Irina picked up her teacup and sipped the cooling tea. —Hey,— Jack said. —Sebastien has something for you.

Irina looked up, blinking as if to bring them back into focus. —Something for me?

—A gift,— Jack said, and with the hand that fell behind Irina's back made a violent gesture at Sebastien's jacket pocket.

Sebastien rolled his eyes, but reached in and produced a black velvet ring box. He set it on the table beside Irina's cup and saucer.

When she looked up, her eyes wide, he nodded. She touched the box lightly, opened it, withdrew the ring and clutched it white-knuckled in her fist. "Thank you."

Jack felt his own cheeks aching when Sebastien smiled. "You know I will not stay in Moscow forever."

She nodded. —I am not sure I will go with you when you leave.

The wampyr looked at Jack. Jack kept his face still as he nodded. Was Sebastien really leaving this up to him?

Apparently.

Sebastien took the nod and turned back to Irina. —I'll come back, when I can.

She lowered her gaze to her knotted fingers. When she opened them, the diameter of the ring was impressed on the flesh of her palm. Her hands shook as she slipped it onto her middle finger.

—It fits,— she said, and burst into tears.

Moscow
Police Palace, Kremlin
May 1903

GARRETT WAS BECOMING MORE fond of Dyachenko than she had anticipated. And it was good, so good to be on the chase again. Garrett had often thought that she was made for one thing—bringing the wicked to justice—and everything else in her life had heretofore been just frills around that main thread.

Now, Kostov dismissed, she remained sitting in Dyachenko's office with him, Sebastien, Phoebe, Irina, and the elder wampyr who had followed Sebastien home and now stood like a statue against the far wall, stony and silent. She almost imagined that she could sense the cold radiating from him. *Is that what Sebastien will be, one day?*

"What next?" Phoebe asked, when the click of the door closing behind Sacha Kostov no longer echoed.

Garrett glanced at Dyachenko. "More interviews?" she hazarded. Police work was police work, the world round.

He nodded—not to her, but to Irina and Starkad. "If we are treating these murders as linked, the logical next step is to work down that list of all your court and associates."

"And those who you spurned," Phoebe said. "I imagine over the years, you did not accept everyone who wanted you."

Garrett did not find Starkad's towering height intimidating. Everything else about him, perhaps, but not his height. Her ingrained response to intimidation was belligerence, and she was priding herself in stepping on the impulse firmly when Starkad smiled at Phoebe. At least, Garrett presumed that was intended a smile—

"You are a writer," Starkad said. "That is good. Not so good as sculpture, but—good. Nonetheless. What you do, it has the potential of persistence." He shrugged. "You are also intelligent and lovely, but that will vanish. What I give my courtiers—is a chance at immortality. If they can clutch it."

Phoebe's chin came up. She said, "And the taste for revolutionaries, sir? Or is that incidental to the art scene? The need to make a mark upon the world?"

The sparkle in dead eyes made it seemed he appreciated spirit, at least. But then, it was usually those with the least grasp on their authority who defended it most vigorously. And this creature—he oozed authority from every pore. Garrett could feel it in her own desire to bring him down a peg or two.

She suspected he'd meet such a sally with equal amusement.

"I find revolutionaries charming," Starkad said. "That is all. In any case, it seems it is not merely three of my former courtiers who have been injured, but four. As Ilya Ilyich Ulyanov was not Sergei's murderer, and Irina was not Lesya's—"

"Then this is an attempt to draw fire upon you and Don Sebastien," Dyachenko said. "And Mrs. Smith's supposition gains in apparent merit."

Sebastien moved, a sudden presence in a room where he had almost in his stillness disappeared—the wampyr gift of seeming no more than a shadow, a coatrack, a glimmer. "It does seem likely that the blood are this killer's targets," he amended. "Or else I would not have been lured to Irina's loft to take the fall for Lesya's murder."

When an answer came to Garrett, it came with such force that she could not believe she had not already seen it. But then—sleep deprivation, a great deal of busyness, and less than forty-eight hours elapsed since Sebastien had been brought in for questioning. It was only the density of events that made it seem like weeks gone by.

"Not the blood," she said. "Irina."

Irina jerked back. "I beg your pardon?"

Garrett started from her chair. It was easier to talk while pacing, even if—in the tight quarters of Dyachenko's office—her skirt brushed the ankles of her allies. "Irina is the common thread. Her lovers, her patrons, her friends. Her canvas. The second murder only occurring when her patron had returned to Moscow and it might seem she was slipping away again. It all leads to a conclusion." She turned abruptly, meeting Irina's gaze. "Was Lesya special to you?"

Irina's lips pressed bloodlessly thin. She glanced aside, and Garrett thought for a moment of reminding her that it was Lesya's killer they were after, and certainly no one in this room was likely to judge someone for whom they loved—but when Garrett refused to look down, Irina nodded tightly and made the leap to courage on her own. "She was."

"The slashed painting?"

"Hers," Irina said. "Of me. She was working in my studio."

Garrett smiled tightly. "So who wants you and cannot have you, Irina Stephanova? And has for the last seven years?"

Irina shook her head, eyes squinched shut. Thinking, Garrett believed. Not hiding inside her head but thinking, thinking grimly, thinking hard.

"Who do you know who is left-handed?" Dyachenko added. He touched Sebastien's note in its folder on his desk. "It's a good forgery of your hand, but this was written by a left-handed person. And Olesia Valentinova was stabbed by a left-handed killer."

This time, Irina did start out of her chair. Now the office was crowded with people moving. Garrett stepped back and resumed her chair as Irina drifted hesitantly to Dyachenko's desk. "A forgery? A *good* forgery?"

Dyachenko blinked. "Does that mean something to you?"

She said, "Well, I know a forger."

—⁂—

In the end, Sebastien accompanied Dyachenko, his henchmen Asimov and the undisgraced Kostov, Starkad, and Abigail Irene—who would no more be left behind on a foray into potential danger than would the terriers she affected—to confront Dmitri. Dmitri Sergeyevich still spent his mornings and afternoons at a café named for kobolds and for cobalt, with the walls still painted that true, bright blue. Sebastien suspected that was how he'd known of Sebastien's return to the city. Irina and Jack had frequented the place. It was only natural that Sebastien should bring his new court there for tea and cookies.

But at night he went home to the flat that had been his mother's, and Irina had been able to tell them where to find it.

Moscow's police did not employ the Black Mariahs made famous by Scotland Yard, but that was only because the Tsar enameled his red and lacquered the Russian eagle in gold upon the doors. Dyachenko ushered Sebastien, Abigail Irene, and Starkad into a similarly gaudy carriage, Kostov driving; behind them Asimov followed with the paddy wagon. The Moscow police used horses of some breed Sebastien imagined derived from the Great Black Horse of memory: heavily feathered even in summer; their dark manes braided atop thick, high-crested necks; their hooves like cake plates in diameter. Not so heavy as a Shire or so stolid as a Percheron, they moved like Frisians but he thought them an older lineage.

They did not rear and fuss when confronted with two wampyrs, but then both Sebastien and Starkad were careful to approach the carriage from the rear.

The ride through night-dark Moscow's muddy streets was all but silent. Dyachenko checked the loads in his revolver. Abby Irene watched out the window, seemingly serene, but Sebastien noticed how she fingered the sleeve where she kept her wand.

Starkad, of course, might as well have been a doll made of papier-mâché over a wire armature. Even in the close confines of the carriage, it was possible to forget his existence for whole minutes at a time.

Instead, Sebastien found his attention drawn to Dyachenko, and the way Abby Irene let her shoulder brush his, once or twice. And the way his pulse reacted when she did.

So, Sebastien thought. *When we have survived this, and there is no conflict of interest. We shall have a word with the good detective then.*

When the carriage pulled up outside Dmitri Sergeyevich's flat, it was Sebastien who reached across the central space to lay his fingertips on Dyachenko's pulsing wrist. "You know that Starkad and I cannot enter his home uninvited."

Dyachenko's eyebrows rose. "I didn't think that was real."

Starkad smiled tightly. "As real as black magic. You must enter first, detective. And we will not be able to help you until you have him out of the flat."

Abby Irene turned her head, summoned from her study. "Unless he flees."

Dyachenko said, "I'll send Kostov and Asimov up the rear stairs."

He might as well not have spoken. Starkad caught Abby Irene's eye and smiled that thing of his that was almost like a smile. "Can you ensure that?"

"Nothing is certain," she said. But her lips curled, and hers was much more like a real smile than anything the wampyr could muster. "Come on. I imagine there are rather a lot of stairs."

It was something to see, a woman in her fifties leading the charge of younger men up four flights, and Sebastien lagged back a little to appreciate it. She ran better than any man could have, in yards of cloth and corsetry, her pale cheeks washed pink and her blue eyes flashing. She was like nothing else, his Abby Irene, and when she was gone there would be nothing to replace or even echo her. Not for the first time, even though he had sworn more than once he would never make another child, Sebastien wished she had ever betrayed an interest in immortality.

But then, she was too smart for that.

Fortuitously, Dmitri must have heard them coming. Because his flat was on the fifth floor, but no one of the blood could have missed the sound of running footsteps down the back stair as they ascended the front, or the moment when Starkad vanished. He was there and then not, and even Sebastien did not sense him leaving.

"Back!" Sebastien cried, and reversed course to the latest landing, at the front of the group now and flying. They would keep up with him as they could; he only thought now was preventing Starkad's vengeance. Starkad's *arbitrary* vengeance; he had no doubt the Tsar's justice would result in much the same result, at least from Dmitri's point of view.

And taking the long view, which was a wampyr's greatest frailty.

He caught the flutter of Starkad's jacket, he thought—or of some cloth, at least, and the cold scent of his fellow in the blood moving inexorable as ice through the passages. "This way!" he cried back, more for Abby Irene than Dyachenko. But he heard the thump of boots and the rustle of broad skirts behind him, and he knew he was leaving them in his dust as surely as had Starkad.

They would catch up when they did. Sebastien's job was to keep Starkad from Dmitri's throat, at least for a little.

Might as well have tried to cage the wind.

But somehow, when he came up on Starkad, the elder held Dmitri one-handed under the chin, his back against the wall and his feet still kicking gently. Sebastien would have presumed his neck broken, but he was familiar with the smell of the gallows, and anyway Dmitri's heart still raced.

—Starkad,— Sebastien said, calmly. —He must stand trial for what he's done.

Starkad turned, so calmly, his eyes pale in his pale face over the russet beard. He must have looked undead even alive. —Of course. How came you to imagine otherwise?

Gently, he lowered Dmitri to his feet. —I will,— he continued, —protect my courtiers. Past and present. But for these purposes, a Russian jail will serve as well as death.

He let a thumb stroke across Dmitri's cheek. —Irina Stephanovna is not for the likes of you.

Dmitri snorted. —What makes you think I ever wanted her? That shallow cow…

Sebastien heard Abby Irene and Dyachenko reach the landing. He stepped forward, pulling Dmitri's attention to him. —So what was it you wanted, then?

Dmitri's head jerked. He glanced aside. His shirt was torn, a bandage ripped back, revealing the marks of human teeth on his right forearm.

Sebastien brushed Starkad's elbow. "You know," he said, "We've been looking at this all wrong."

Two more sets of footsteps closing. One would be Kostov, the other Asimov. *Time's up.*

Except not quite, because Starkad was looking at him with interest, and the humans were drawing up a good ten feet off, leaving the wampyrs to their victim.

The humans, that is to say, except for Abigail Irene.

Heels clicking, she pushed past Dyachenko's restraining arm and stalked up to stand beside Sebastien, her ebony wand glinting in its silver fittings and her brow thunderous. "What did he say?"

Starkad stepped back, withdrawing outside the immediate circle. His body, Sebastien realized, was a barrier for the policemen now.

Quickly, Sebastien translated, and watched Abby Irene's wrath turn to irritation. He was simultaneously aware of surrounding events—Dyachenko's breath quickening at Abby Irene's forthright purpose, Asimov forcing himself to step back and observe when his every instinct was to tackle.

"He doesn't care about Irina," Abby Irene said. "Are you blind? This is all about your colleague."

Her nod indicated Starkad; Starkad (without releasing his grip on Dmitri) looked at her in surprise—for once, his emotions transparent on that ancient face.

"Yes," Abby Irene said. "You. Oi, Dmitri Sergeyevich. Sebastien, if you please?"

"Translate?"

She smiled. "You know me so well. Please."

He cleared his throat, then, and spoke for the lady.

Abigail Irene said, and Sebastien said for her, —A forger but a poor artist. Starkad never really looked at you, did he?

Dmitri would not answer, but his jaw firmed and his eyes drifted up. His hands clenched.

As if it were ripped from him, he said, over Sebastien's shoulder, —You would not...you would not give me a ring.

Starkad might have been a statue, for all he showed the pain Sebastien could smell in him. —And so you took Ilya's? Before or after you had him executed?

Dmitri turned his head away, jaw working.

Softly, Starkad said —You never made anything that would last. You were never more than a copyist to Irina, to Ilya. Even Sergei was better.

Dmitri closed his eyes. —Don't you think I tried?

—I think trying is not enough,— Starkad said.

—Don't you think I tried with everything in me? Don't you think I...

He shuddered, a pain as deep as if someone had sunk a knife in his belly. —Your court, the rest of your court, you bastard. *That,*— and his finger shook as he pointed at Sebastien. —None of that is going to last forever. What power do you have? Look at *me*. Take me seriously, love me, *kill* me. Or I'll leave you with nothing but a *wasteland*.

Starkad did not step back, though Sebastien imagined in the elder's shoes, he might have. —So.

He looked left, at Sebastien and Abby Irene, and behind them Dyachenko. He looked right, where stood Asimov and Kostov.

And then he shrugged and turned away, leaving Dmitri shouting at his back, near-incoherently.

Dmitri lunged, and Dyachenko's pistol swung to follow him. But Abby Irene's wand was in her hand, and Dmitri met the floor face-first instead of ever reaching Starkad.

Sebastien hurried to catch up with the other wampyr, while Abby Irene and Dyachenko's officers converged on Dmitri. "So."

"So," Starkad answered.

"You didn't kill him."

Starkad shrugged. "No. I did not."

"You owe him for four deaths."

"Five. And a painting."

It was rude to keep pushing, quite outside the bonds of the blood's hierarchy to ask. But for all his years, Sebastien could not help himself. "So why let the Tsar have him?"

By the stairs, Starkad stopped and looked at him. Patiently, as if to a slow child, he said: "He will be over soon."

Moscow
Bely Gorod
January 1897

WHEN JACK CAME HOME——IF you could call their cheap flat *home*, exactly—it was several hours after sunset, and the last thing he expected was Sebastien waiting at the kitchen table with his knitting and a book. As Jack let himself in and locked the door behind himself, the wampyr arose.

"Out with your revolutionary friends?" he asked. "You know they are hanging that boy Ilya tomorrow."

Jack nodded. "I was with Irina."

"I see," said Sebastien. He was a slender, darker shape against the darkness, something fragile and as real as a knife blade. He took a breath, deep enough that Jack heard the rare inhalation, and continued: "They fight against the government, they fight for rights and wages, they fight as if it mattered. And for what? In a hundred years, it will not matter. This will all dry up and blow away."

He is old, Jack told himself. *He is old and in pain.*

"It matters," Jack said, "now."

Sebastien stopped like a clockwork run out to the end. It was a long time before he spoke, and when he did his tones were low and bitter. "He was a boy, and he'll hang."

"That's the world."

"Facile," Sebastien said. "Your cynicism."

Jack crossed the kitchen. He put a hand on the wampyr's arm. He snaked fingers through Sebastien's black hair and tried to tug him down to press his face into the crook of Jack's shoulder, but it was like bending iron.

"Come to bed, Sebastien."

"You will only leave me."

Jack smiled, though Sebastien's tone of resignation made him feel as though the space around his heart had been sewed up.

"Probably," he said. "Unless you leave me first. But despite all that, sweetheart. I love you."

He kissed the wampyr, and the wampyr did not push him away.

Moscow
Bely Gorod
May 1903

STARKAD'S LAIR, BY RIGHTS, should have been hard to find. It should have been well-concealed, near-impossible to track.

Sebastien simply followed him.

He stayed in an old loft over a warehouse, where—as no one lived there but a wampyr—Sebastien could enter without invitation.

Enter, but not go unnoticed. And what he pursued was unto him as he was unto any merely human member of his court.

In a human heartbeat, Sebastien found himself pinned against the wall beside the door. Starkad bent over him, the chill of his flesh emanating, his smile so close by Sebastien's skin that Sebastien could feel the way the air moved between them. When he spoke, his words stirred the fine hairs on Sebastien's throat. The language was old and softly spoken, full of hushed shirring sounds, as dear and half-forgotten as a cradle song.

Were Sebastien mortal, he would have clenched his fists to still wracking shivers. Undead, he merely stood still—so still—and waited, while Starkad murmured the words of a medieval poem against his ear.

"Your mother tongue," Starkad whispered when he was done—still in the old Galician, a few hundred years newer than the words Sebastien had been raised on, but close, so close—so much closer than anything he had heard in all the centuries since. "How long has it been since you heard it, Lopo?"

Sebastien had to go down a long way, and come a long way back, to find the words to answer. "Whose name is that, Starkardr?"

It was a mundane, a common name. The name of a laborer. So familiar.

"Yours," the wampyr answered. His cold hand stroked Sebastien's cold cheek, the flesh so very thin between their bones. "How have you come to have forgotten it, child of Eudaline, when it is so easy for me to recall?"

"I have forgotten a great deal," Sebastien said. "What did not die with the years died with my maker."

"Mmm." Starkad's dry lips brushed his skin. Reflexively, Sebastien turned his head, baring his throat to one so much elder and more powerful. The blood were at their very heart the most hierarchical of creatures. Desire was a cramp inside him, hard enough to arch his body to a painful comma. He fought it; all his strength bent on standing straight. On not humiliating himself before the elder.

The elder who said, "But I know it, and I will give it back to you. Your name is Lopo."

Most wampyrs smelled faintly sweetish in death, an attar of sugar, salt, and the metal of the blood by which they lived. Starkad smelled of—nothing, or almost nothing. Salt mud crazed in cold weather. Round stones sheened by the ice of a winter river. Sebastien breathed it deep, dragging a dead scent across dead senses. It was a relief not to be the old one, for a change. Not to set the tone of every encounter. It would have been even more of a relief to surrender—

"I cannot return the gift," Sebastien said. "The language of your mortal years was lost long before I could have learned it."

"I take no offense," Starkad said. "You cannot be held accountable for what faded before you were born. I am eldest; knowledge is my burden. But your tongue, I can give you. Your tongue, and your name. Here, child, have it of me. You are Lopo of no father, Lopo the Moor's bastard. In the blood, you are the child of Eudaline."

The pause was so portentous, Sebastien knew almost to a certainty what would follow.

Until Starkad said, "And I am the Norseman, child of Gaius."

The surprise was so much that at first he thought he heard what he expected, and he jerked back against the cup of Starkad's hand that had somehow come to rest against his skull. "*Gaius?*"

"You thought I would say another name."

"If you were Evie's blood brother—it would explain how you knew of me, when I should be nothing of significance to you." The knowledge came with a pang of loss.

Starkad's breath was cold against Sebastien's lips. Sebastien fought the urge to lick them with a dry cold tongue, as if licking up the elder's scent. He failed.

"I am not your grandsire Aethelwyn's child. I was born before even he. But you lived longer than most of the young ones, and so did your dam. I made it my business to learn."

Sebastien found himself relaxing into the embrace of long fingers cradling his skull. Starkad's body pressed his own; the elder felt light and hard and unimaginably strong. Sebastien knew what he would be like under his clothes, a shape of twisted silk cable and dry cold supple leather like calfskin.

"Like the art," Sebastien said. Starkad's nostrils flared on *his* breath, in return. The tension between them was sublimating, turning to vapor, saturating the air all around. It was becoming inevitable, what would happen, and that inevitability brought a kind of peace.

Sebastien already knew that he would not deny Starkad what the elder so patently desired. He desired it too, this thing he had not had since Eudaline burned. Surrender. To not be the one who was accountable.

"Like the art," Starkad admitted. "You—" he laughed, dry and soft, his breath moving the ruddy strands of his beard "—you might outlast me."

"Is that why you want me?"

"You need a better court," Starkad said. "Two is too few. A dozen, that would be better. The police detective likes you, and he likes your sorceress. You should prey upon him."

"Are you my tutor?"

Starkad smiled. "You seem to need one, though you are old for the schoolhouse."

"Answer the question, then. Why is it that you want me, who could have anyone?"

"You persist. I need such things, such anchors, if I am to endure." He pressed a finger to Sebastien's lips.

Sebastien, without averting his eyes from Starkad's transparent ones, let his tongue drift out to taste the soft, dead flesh that barely cloaked the bone. He watched those water-sapphire eyes drift closed and thought *He will leave me too. He wishes to be the one who leaves this time. After a while, it is more than we can bear to be left, again and again and again, by lovers. By the world. By history. He will leave me. Like Eudaline.*

He took a breath for speaking with. "What is your name, then, old one?"

"Starkardr," he said. "When I stopped playing the human game, I stopped having reasons to lie." Gently, he let his lips brush Sebastien's.

Because it seemed a statement out of experience rather than an oblique insult—Starkad was out of any doubt beyond obliqueness—Sebastien, lightly, kissed him back.

—⚭—

It had been a long time since Sebastien surrendered to something more powerful than he.

It was surprisingly easy, in the end.

—⚭—

"Starkardr?"

"I am listening."

"And what was the name of Aethelwyn-sire-of-Eudaline's sire?"

The silence was answer enough. *Old, yes. Old beyond imagining.*

After it had persisted a while, Sebastien brought in air to speak again. "I can do you the service you desire."

Silence again, and no denial. But a pause before Starkad answered, "What service is that, my darling Lopo?"

If Sebastien had a heart that beat, it would have been straining the bonds of his chest just then. "You can be the one who leaves. This time. With me. I will wait as long as you need me."

"You cannot promise that."

"Oh," Sebastien said. "I do."

Silence.

When Sebastien turned his head, the other side of the bed was empty and cold. He had never felt the wampyr rise.

Sebastien rose too, and smoothed his hair without benefit of the mirror. Enough brief night remained to return to the hotel in safety, if he was quick about it.

Dyachenko and his meager court would be awaiting him. And Starkad was right; It was a shortfall in need of addressing.

"I'll see you again," Sebastien said through the crack to the empty room, before he shut the door.

Intently though he listened, there came no answer.